someone
should
pay for
your pain

Portions of this book originally appeared, in different forms,
at Punknews.org and in the anthology *Waiting To Be Forgotten* (Gutter Press).

This is a work of fiction. Any resemblance to actual persons or events is coincidental.

GIBSON HOUSE PRESS
Flossmoor, Illinois
GibsonHousePress.com

ISBNs: 978-1-948721-13-4 (paperback); 978-1-948721-14-1 (ebook)

LCCN: 2020941734

Cover and text design by Karen Sheets de Gracia
Text is set in Cardea.

someone should pay for your pain

a novel

FRANZ NICOLAY

GIBSON HOUSE PRESS

CHICAGO

Teach us to care and not to care
Teach us to sit still.

—T. S. Eliot, "Ash-Wednesday"

part I

1

(2018)

THE KID WANTED so much not to be the bad guy.

"Hey Rudy, can I talk to you about the money?"

Here it comes, Rudy thought. I'm gonna get the dictionary definition of "guarantee" tattooed on my damn arm.

"Listen, I know I said five hundred in the email. But, I just thought, you know, we got some good write-ups, and it's winter up here and not much is going on."

The kid also wanted so much not to lose money. That's what these guys first learn when they decide they want to be promoters. You can be liked or you can make money.

"I thought it was a good turnout, right? I've got $375, can we do that?"

"Five hundred," said Rudy. "Matter of fact, as I recall, the offer for the original date was eight. It's a seven-hour drive to get here. I took off work."

"I guess I could go to an ATM." He paused, waiting for Rudy to say, *Oh, you don't have to do that.*

Rudy waited back.

"I guess—" The mercy might yet come. "I just—I was really excited to have you come. It's a big deal for me. For my promotion company. I want you to be happy, and let people know that you had a good show here."

"I appreciate that."

"I—" He sagged, punctured. "I'll be right back. I'll get some money out of my own account."

"That is often how it's done," Rudy agreed.

RUDY HAD DRIVEN up that morning, from the flat part of New York State that looked more like Nebraska. The dry snow blew in feathered gusts across the pitted highway. Some autodidact homesteader had scattered place-names from Plutarch and Thucydides, which clanged, now, against the shambling barns and the broad accents. He had a short weekend of shows—Montreal, Toronto—then a slow drive across the sallow belly of the continent. His father had emailed asking him to take a few days off after Toronto and visit the cabin, but he hadn't responded. Hope that gig comes through in Vancouver, then stay at the group house in Bellingham. Do a couple weeks of drywalling at the farm in Idaho where he picked up seasonal construction work, or renew his CDL and get a route to Tallahassee. Everyone he knew in Winnipeg and Fargo had moved to Minneapolis and then to Chicago, so motel nights there. Too cold to sleep in the car.

For that matter, he didn't know anyone in Montreal, either. But it was easy to find a place to stay if you were just one guy. Worst-case scenario, just throw it out there from stage—*hey, I need a spot tonight*—and see who bites. Get some pleasant surprises that way.

If the towns behind him were antiquarian fantasy, those by the border were alphabet gumbo: Chazy, Sciota, Ausable. Imaginary but plausible words you'd fake a definition for in an after-dinner game. It was easy, these days, to get into Canada. Once upon a time, when shows were bigger and there were more people in the car, a touring party could depend on getting all their merch counted, customs duties assessed, documents swabbed for residue, in case you kept your passport in your pocket with your packet. And God forbid anyone had an old DUI—have to cancel a week's worth of shows. But in the old Timonium with a guitar, a box of CDs, and a suitcase, he got waved through. A raised eyebrow at the mattress in the back. How long you staying, have a nice trip.

Montreal was always farther from the border than Rudy expected. After the brief thrill of the crossing—is the phone in airplane mode, what ticket from Speedtrap, Georgia, did I tear up three years ago—he felt like he ought to be there already. But another forty-five minutes of highway remained, and the scrubbed crust of wind-sculpted snow dunes on the shoulder; then the undulating bridge, the skeletal amusement park, and the old brick city.

Two hours, still, until sound check. He pulled over at a coffee chain. In your own town, he thought, this place is the soulless hole that put Hippie Mike's Uncommon Groundz out of business; get two hours away and it's a beacon of free Wi-Fi. He tempered a charred coffee with half-and-half and pulled out his laptop. A sticker reading "Mountain Music Museum, Kingsport, Tennessee" covered the logo on the scuffed black plastic shell. The computer whirred, flashed, and chimed.

> Hi Rudy—
> I'm very excited to see your show tonight! *The Morris Column* is one of my favorite records. I'm sure you're busy, but if you need a place to kill some time or a hot meal, I live fifteen minutes from the venue, feel free to hit me up!
> xo,
> James

Rudy's lower lip tensed into a stillborn smile: a fleeting gratitude, shooed by the anticipation of a filthy collegiate couch, an all-night "hang," and questions about Ryan Orland. Also, what kind of sign-off was "xo" between two men who didn't know each other?

> Hi James—
> As it happens, I do need a place to stay. I'm in town. Can I come by? Where do you live? You don't have a cat, do you?
> R

He sipped his coffee and rebuttoned his quilted jacket. The top buttonhole was stretched beyond usefulness by this fidget, which, in turn, made the tic near-constant. The computer dinged.

> Rudy!
> No cats. I'm at 1132 Côte-de-porcs. No phone, ring the bell when you get here.
> James

It was late winter. Judging by the streets, the city had a laissez-faire policy toward snow removal. The slush had frozen, melted, and refrozen into a grimy, rutted scarp. He drove with care to the front of James's building, then yanked the wheel, the car spinning and skidding over the berm left by the plows. It would pass for parked.

Rudy crumped over the snowbank and knocked at the door, twice. It opened.

"Yes?" An ectomorph in a bright wool hat with a pom-pom, a cardigan and boxer shorts, bare feet in wool-lined slippers; inquisitive but immobile, as if he were a troll—questions three—set to guard the door.

"Is James here?"

"He is inside": a central European accent.

"I'm meeting him. May I come in?"

His greeter stepped aside, and retreated upstairs. Next to the mat lay five boots. Not five pairs, just five boots.

Three young people sat on a collection of misfit couches, which partitioned sitting room from kitchen. One—Bernard, accent on the first syllable, had a clean pink face and pants that only reached his calves; next, Claire, slim with short hair and wide teeth. The third, blond with a British accent, introduced himself as James from the email, an exchange student from the north of England. He showed Rudy upstairs, and waved a hand toward a bunk bed. "You can sleep here. I put fresh sheets on it and everything." He giggled. "It's the most grown-up thing I've done in weeks."

"Appreciate it," said Rudy. "But where will you stay?"

"I can put down a mat in the hallway. It'll just be one night for me. You do this every night."

Rudy grumbled a combination thanks and apology. "How many people live here?"

"Eight, counting me." They returned downstairs to the front room. "Would you like some soup?" He ladled a bowl of bloody beets from a ten-gallon pot, and ripped off a thick chunk of steaming sourdough.

This time, Rudy gave him a grunt of simple gratitude. "How do you like it here?" he asked. "How's your French?"

"Not great," said James. "Anyway, the French girls scare me. You go to a party and they'll be smoking indoors, and saying things like, 'If you like me, go punch that guy over there.'"

"We are playing a game," said Bernard. One of the only remaining signifiers of class in North America, Rudy thought looking at his crossed legs, is young men who wear loafers with no socks. "You tell a story that you improve with a lie, and then you confess the lie. I already went."

"That's a lie," said James. "But his stories are boring, so that's the improvement."

"I've never lied," offered Claire. She drew her knees up to her chin.

"How about you?" James asked Rudy.

"Constantly," said Rudy. "People prefer it. They'd rather have your story be half-true and funny. Plenty of the time it's even immoral not to lie."

"But you're a songwriter," said James. "Songs can't help but tell the truth, don't you think?"

It is desperately easy for music to lie, is what Rudy wanted to say, to be made and consumed in bad faith. Most of what people think is truth is just cliché, something they've heard so many times they figure there must be a reason. Truth isn't a necessary quality for a story. "I once met this guy who claimed to be in a biker gang," he said, "which, fine, if you say so. I said what's your motto. He said, 'The real risk is in the coming home.' Nice line. C'mon, though."

"I've never lied," Claire insisted again.

Rudy excused himself and slipped upstairs.

HE COULD TELL the sound guy had decided he hated him before Rudy had even finished uncoiling his cables. This one had a pudgy face under choppy hair dyed black, and a baby beer gut hanging over his street-vendor studded belt. Motherfucker, I've been doing this longer than you've been alive. Don't roll your eyes at me over the talk-back.

The room, of course, was black. Plywood, spray-painted. Band stickers in the urinals. Anyone he'd heard of? No one you ever hear of puts their stickers in urinals.

This room did have a skate ramp next to the stage. That was a new one.

"We're really excited to have you," the promoter said. "I'm a big Ryan Orland fan, and I saw you on a list of his favorite song-writers, so I checked you out. You see much of him?"

"Well," said Rudy, "his label puts out my records. He used to come to my shows when he was a teenager. I let him open a couple times."

"But you used to tour together, right? You know, you guys sound a lot alike."

"That's what they say."

"What'd you think of his new record?"

"I guess it's alright. I don't really—" He looked past the promoter, down the stairs. "Where's a good place to get a beer?"

"You get half off two domestics at the bar here."

"Where else?"

HE SHOULDN'T HAVE had fries with that burger. And the drinks. The one made him sleepy, the other touchy. It was almost midnight. Show running late. Doors hadn't been until 9:30 and there were three openers: a guy in a flannel shirt pretending something about whiskey. An ethereal blonde, seated, capoed high and trilling higher. Someone with an accordion missing the point of a waltz.

By the time Rudy plugged in, he'd already decided the crowd would hate his show—which made it almost a certainty. Mostly teenage couples in hoodies and jeans, on quasi-dates with other friends. A couple of boys sitting up on the half-pipe shared a water bottle, which was pretty clearly filled with something else, because who shares a bottle of water?

"Hello," he said into the mic. "I'm Rudy Pauver." People always looked surprised at his speaking voice, high and sweet, left over from a younger and more vulnerable body. He began:

I saw your picture on the Morris column
Half still stuck, half ripped and fallen

His singing voice was even more incongruous, a quavering, bruised vibrato on the verge of cracking.

A month gone, longer forgotten
A missed connection, a lost dog howling

Once they acclimated to his soft canine moan, they could fill in the gaps between the gentleness in their ears and the rough man in their eyes. They noticed his broad, delicate lips, his eyes set just a bit wide, disappearing in a face gone puffy. And his stance, not a big man's wide confidence, but top-heavy, feet drawn close and a little pigeon-toed, shoulders hunched over his guitar as he picked with thick fingers.

I threw a crumb to a pigeon, it stared as if to say
"Don't look to me for thanks, my people ruled this place

A girl up front whispered something to her boyfriend, not softly enough. Rudy shook his head like a bull trying to shoo troublesome flies.

We've grown small and soft with feathers, but I remember
Drag my dinner from the trash, and call it treasure."

There was a crash and a rolling clatter. What the fuck. Was the bartender really choosing this time to empty the recycling?

He stopped the song short and turned—no, not recycling.

The boys with the bottle had passed judgment on him from the top of the half-pipe and turned away from the stage. One sprang to his feet—still bent at the waist, hunched under the ceiling—and dropped in. The wheels rumbled on the plywood.

The high whine in his brain drowned out the song—his first, or fourth, or twentieth. His tongue went slippery, the words like unsupervised toddlers, whoops, he tried to grab them, but they'd thrown themselves down the slide, pointing and crying, I broke it, Daddy, fix it.

"YOU TOLD THE promoter to go fuck himself," James said helpfully the next morning. "Actually, first, you unplugged your guitar and packed it up. Then you turned back to the mic and told the audience that you hoped their dreams would curdle and that they would live long enough to regret their joys as much as their mistakes. Then you walked out the front door. I don't know how you found your way here, or got in, but you were asleep by the time we got back. The other two are on a blanket in the hall, careful you don't step on them."

2

EXIT-RAMP RETAIL CLUSTER, western Quebec. On his first Canadian tour, he'd been excited to have a cup of Tim Horton's coffee—local flavor, and the gentle gratification of a stereotype fulfilled, like seeing a guy with a Maple Leafs patch on his earflap hat. Now it just gave him a nostalgic shiver: this is what coffee used to taste like, before strong coffee went nationwide. Like drinking the water they used to rinse the espresso machine.

He opened the trunk to pull his driving glasses from his bag. He'd bought a pair of novelty sunglasses at a Flying J in Oklahoma, plastic bug eyes bedazzled along the temples. Took them to the mall shop and had them put in prescription lenses. They pretend they can't do that, so you'll buy name-brand frames, but they will. It helped get him in the right mindset for long drives.

A woman in a Subaru rolled down the passenger window and yelled something in French about "*le cinema.*"

He walked over to her window. "You mind if I speak English?" he asked. She shook her head. "I passed a movie theater back that way about a half-mile, if that's what you're looking for."

She waved thank you. He turned back to his car.

"Learn some fuckin' French!" she shouted at his back, and pulled out of the lot.

CANADAS BEST VALUE INN. No apostrophe. Four words, three lies.

The innkeeper, a thin, balding man, was asleep under a blanket on the lobby couch. Rudy brought a six-pack, and cold fries in a Styrofoam clamshell, to his room. He stacked three of the meager pillows and lay back against the detached headboard. The mattress slid forward. He cursed, got up, pushed the mattress back against the wall—better not to look in that gap—and propped a table against the foot of the bed. He crawled back under the sheet and opened his laptop. *You got a nice write-up for the Vancouver show*, wrote Rose from the label. He clicked the link. The local free rag had lifted an old promo shot off of the internet: thirty pounds lighter, cheekbones, jean jacket, a wool hat pulled down to his brow. Smiling, even. Cass behind the camera, he remembered. They'd sleep, the two of them, coiled on the back seat of the van. *Now my charms are all o'erthrown.*

> Ryan Orland protégé Rudy Pauver comes to the Sail Away Thursday night, still touring behind his last record, *The Ritual Slaughter of Rudy Pauver,* on Orland's Bad Dream imprint. Once bassist for the Gainesville, Florida-based hardcore band Expatriate Games, Pauver's reinvention as a troubadour has been called "an inspiration" by the young indie heartthrob, and fans of the latter will find much to like at Pauver's show (tickets should be easier to get, too).
>
> **The Sail Away, Monday. Doors 8pm, show 9pm. $8, adv $5. All ages.**

Rudy closed the laptop. Lights flashed through the curtains. A woman's yell dopplered by, as a car pulled out of the parking lot with an animal squeal.

RUDY PULLED BEHIND a Petro-Canada in eastern Saskatchewan and parked by a concrete-shoed lamppost. Snowdrifts chased each other across the glistening parking lot and broke on the sides of trucks. He'd gotten ice in his shoe at the last filling station, and his right sock was clammy and cold. He opened the trunk, then his suitcase, to pull out a dry pair. The rear of the car was scaly with road salt.

"Hey! Hey bud! Excuse me!"

Rudy panned upwards, saw a pair of construction boots, baggy stonewashed jeans, a khaki vest over a gray hoodie, a Labrador-blond moustache, a bright orange beanie.

"Hey man, you need a hand?"

Rudy shook his head no. "I'm OK, thanks."

"You sure? Where you from? North Carolina?"

"Just the plates," said Rudy.

"I work here. Just want to—we've had thieves around here. Gotta watch your laptop. You got a computer, probably."

"Just stopping for a second to get some socks."

"Alright, just trying to help. Guitar, huh? You a musician?"

"Yup."

His eager demeanor hardened. "You need any weed?"

Rudy put both hands on the edge of the trunk. He looked at his three wrinkled, folded shirts, and the toothpaste tube in a Ziploc. His shoulders drooped a little. "No, thank you. I haven't smoked in years."

"Oh yeah?" The man stood up straighter. Shed his doggishness. "What kind of musician doesn't do drugs? If I call my guys and search your car we won't find anything?"

Rudy closed the suitcase and turned to face him. "I thought you said you worked here."

"I do."

"You're a cop."

Blank stare.

"If you really, truly, absolutely must, you can tear this fucking car apart. I'll go eat a fucking burger, and then another one and a milkshake just for fun. I'll move the fuck in here and shit in the truckers' shower. While you look for weed in my car."

A walkie-talkie crackled in one stonewashed back pocket. The man grabbed it with his left hand without taking his eyes off Rudy: "Yeah. Back lot. Honda." A pickup truck pulled out, fast, from around the truckstop corner. His right hand came out from his vest pocket, with a knife.

"Goddamn it. Really?"

RUDY SAT IN the diner booth and picked at the grimy, fungal foam that poked through a rip in the vinyl seat. They'd taken the bag, which meant the laptop. His phone buzzed—Rose. Not now, Rose. Luckily, if you could say that, half of the five hundred from Toronto had already gone to gas and the motel.

But the passport, the fucking passport. A man without a country, after all this time. Finally go expat. At least this was Canada; the embassy was probably like a Montessori school. Maybe get a tune out of it. If your only tool is a guitar, every problem sounds like a song.

The phone buzzed again, scuffling sideways across the Formica like a sand crab. Jozef, from the bar. Rudy had weekend shifts back home, up till four waiting for coke vampires to stroke half-drunk Coronas for an hour. Dammit Jozef, I told you I'd call you when I got back.

The phone scuttled all the way around the coffee cup this time, headed straight for the ketchup. What the fuck, somebody set off a bomb in Times Square or something? He flipped the phone open. "Jesus, what?"

"Hey Rudy, it's Rose. Good news or bad news first?"

Rudy stuck a fry upright in the bun of his burger. Happy birthday to somebody, probably. "All news is bad news."

"Whatever. The Vancouver show isn't happening. The kid who said he'd put it on was getting squirrelly, he wanted to switch to a door deal, and now I haven't heard from him for ten days."

"Fuck. Fuck! I need that show. You know what just happened to me? I got rolled at a rest stop."

"What? Anyway, but check it out—Ryan has a song about you on his new record. 'The Ballad of Rudy Pauver.' It might be the single."

Rudy looked out the window. Two boys in puffy trash-bag coats were tussling. One pulled away and drew a dick in the slushy back window of an Econoline van.

"You there? This is good for you, Rudy."

"He could have just covered 'Morris Column' or something. At least that way I'd make some money on it." He pulled at the skin over his cheekbone. "I don't want to be a legend, I want to be solvent."

"Oh, come on. It's a compliment. A gesture, like. He's trying to help."

He blew his nose in a napkin and stuffed it into the coffee cup. It shrank, soggy and brown.

"Just keep driving to Vancouver and come over to the office. Ryan has a house across the bay. He's on tour, but you can stay there as long as you need. I'll get you the code."

SUBURBS. PRICEY SUBURBS, but still. This must be the house for when Ryan wanted to relax into lawnmowing-dad drag for a couple weeks. Tough work, to be a member of pop culture's idle class. Tall white fence, black aluminum security gate. Punch in the code: 3-1-2-1. The gate whirred to the left.

"Can I help you?" A kid with greased-over black hair, tight black jeans, and a flannel button-down, leaned out the door. "This is a private residence."

"I'm Rudy. I'm on Bad Dream. Rose gave me the code, said I could stay here tonight."

"Oh." He stood aside, but didn't offer his name or his hand. "OK."

The house looked like the seventies trophy playground of a hip stockbroker or publisher of a successful magazine. Ryan must have dug the rocker rec-room vibe. The original shag. No renovations. In fact, it was barely furnished. The suburban whim must not strike that often.

In the meantime, the house apparently served as a crash pad for a small cross section of the local bohemian elite, a half-dozen of whom were strewn in a frieze of languor on the couches and rug around the low living-room table. They regarded Rudy with the resentful defensiveness of teenagers whose parents have come home early.

"There's a free room down there, third door on the right." The kid gestured to a hall. "Bathroom's across the way."

"Thanks. What's your name?" Rudy stuck out his hand.

"Oh. Sorry. I'm Brendan, I look after the place for Ryan when he's away."

"Keep the rugs clean and the pipes from freezing."

"Something like that. Do you know Connor from Dictation?" Dictation was another Bad Dream act. Post-something. Not terrible. A skinny guy with horn-rimmed glasses wider than his temples waved hello and lit a slim joint off a columnar candle.

"You the new bass player?" Rudy asked.

"Yeah, for a couple years now."

"Davey D. still in the band?"

"He's guitar tech-ing for Deaf Moon. He'll be back in a few weeks. You want some of this?"

Rudy set his backpack on a wall-length shelf, next to the plastic suitcase turntable. He took the joint and a hit.

Connor introduced the others—a freelance music writer, a guy who fixed amps at the guitar shop, a booker at one of the local rock boxes. Middlemen and hangers-on.

"There's beer in the fridge if you want some," Brendan said. "Jameson on the counter."

"Rudy, yeah?" said the writer. "Rudy Pauver?"

Rudy nodded.

"Is that your car out there?" said guitar-store guy. "You sleep in that thing?"

"Sometimes," said Rudy. "Hot in the summer, cold in the winter."

Guitar guy shook his head. "Man. I couldn't do that. I'm a homebody, I guess. I like my bed and my cats."

Rudy took a bottle of beer from the fridge, looked for an opener, and levered off the cap with a nearby bottle of olive oil. He pulled a plastic Smurfs cup from the dish drainer and poured some whiskey.

"What're you up to?" asked the writer. "*Morris Column* was pretty big for you, right?"

"That was fifteen years ago, though," said Rudy. "I've done, what, five since? Got a new record out a few months ago."

"Oh yeah? I gotta check that out. Hey, did I read something today about Ryan writing a song about you?"

"I guess so."

"Maybe that'll get you out of that car."

Rudy got up. "I'm going to turn in. Nice to meet you all." He started to leave, then stopped and filled the Smurfs cup to the brim.

HE AWOKE PAST midnight, sweaty on a brand-new but unmade mattress. He'd turned his jacket inside out, made a pillow of the lamb's-wool lining. He had to pee. Where was the light? Patted his way around the wall. Hallucinated woozy swirls in the dark. There was the door handle. Hallway light. Now which door was the fucking bathroom? He tried one. Silhouetted against a headboard, Connor from whatever band rolled over and blinked.

"Sorry," Rudy muttered. Got it the next try. Swayed a little over the toilet, missed a little too. Give that kid Brendan something to do. Caretaker. Good gig. I'd take care of this place. Take care of it real good.

The party had left a candle burning, a pungent hippie pillar. Rudy grabbed it. See where I'm going at least. Back to the bedroom. Where can I put this thing? No nightstand. No furniture at all. Just the white shag and the bed, and a few boxes of Ryan T-shirts. Using this room for label storage. Pack me away here, too, with all the other merch that won't sell. For posterity. Wait till I'm vintage. That's me, pre-worn. Distressed.

Set the candle on one of the boxes. Let me look at this shit. Open the cross-folded cardboard leaves. Ryan's shy, dimpled grin in high contrast, on cotton, folded flat. Soft. Not that Gildan shit. Was that a beard? What a joke. Trying to look serious. Can't have a serious face if you've been famous since you were a teenager.

Rudy stumbled and fell back against the bed, breathing heavily, his mouth open. Kneed the tower of boxes as he went down. Hot wax on fabric. Ryan's face curling away.

3

EVERY HANGOVER IS alike; every hangover is miserable in its own way. How many hangover scenes will this life have, was Rudy's first thought. It's a disgrace. Worse, it's boring.

The fire, was his second thought. Ah Jesus shit, the fire. Half a box of shirts was charred through, but it looked like the rest of them had fallen over and snuffed it out. Weightless black flakes floated and shifted, but the carpet wasn't even singed.

Mostly what he felt was a vague disappointment. Rudy had never actively considered killing himself—people who did weren't just depressed and angry, but despairing; they were the ones who couldn't blame anyone but themselves. Rudy still had a few go-to scapegoats. A good grudge was enough to keep you alive. Suicide was just a comforting idea to have on hand, a threat to keep his mind in line: you keep it down, don't make me come in there. Eventually he would have a new idea for a song he was, more or less, glad of, and the songs skimmed the scum off his brain before it got too thick.

Still, the fire felt like a missed opportunity.

Rudy brushed the cover from his legs, swung them off the bed and into the swath of ashes. He rubbed one blackened sole on the opposite calf, smearing both.

Brendan and some of the others were still in the living room, still reclined, now softly wheezing and snoring. They could caretake the ashes. Rudy rinsed the Smurf cup and set it, without a sound, in the drying rack. He held the doorknob retracted as he closed the door.

The consulate, as he'd expected, was polite and efficient, and he had a temporary passport in under an hour. He drove south across the border, pulled off in Blaine, and turned his phone back on. It buzzed gently in his hand.

uncle r, read the gray screen. *i saw u were coming to seattle. im here too. can u help me out. oh this is lily btw*

Rudy wiped his hand down his face from brow to beard. He gathered a fist as he passed his Adam's apple, then shoved both palm-heels into his eye sockets and held them there.

part II

4

(1999)

CASS AND RUDY found each other at a house party in Augusta. Rudy had tagged along with a friend's band. Jump in the van and sell merch, just five hours up the coast, why not? Meet some people, stay at their musty Victorian, try to find a couch to sleep on, tingle your asshole in the shower with a stranger's Dr. Bronner's. Tire-sized rolls of brittle toilet paper, filched twice weekly from the one broken dispenser on campus that still got restocked. One wall covered from wainscoting to trim with empty record sleeves. The crusties ran together in a wash—maybe that wasn't the word—of olive and patches and dreadlocks and serrated, steel-wool voices: *I'm Hogtie, and this*—dirty mutt, defeated ears—*is Bacon. He barks when he sees cops, that's why I call him Bacon. This is my buddy Barbecue. I don't know, I think he had a barbecue once.*

Cass had a dyed-black pageboy, and a white rat on the shoulder of her motorcycle jacket. She'd painted a slogan, or a cartoon, who could remember, now cracked and peeling, on the leather back. She kept putting the rat's head in her mouth as a kind of party trick. Rudy had a flop of sand-dune hair over his right eye and a high bashful voice. He kept fussing with the cuffs of his shirt—a plain long-sleeved button-down fastened at the wrists, even in the southern summer house-show heat. He told her how, in elementary school, he put a note in a sandwich bag and tied it to a helium balloon; let it off and got a letter two months later from two states away. She told him how she, immune, used to use poison ivy leaves as page markers so no one would borrow her books. He told her no one would lend him books anymore because he dog-eared the pages, and that it was too loud in this room. She told him about the first boy who tried to French kiss her, backstage at their fifth-grade play: she was dressed as the ghost from Hamlet; she punched him in the chest and told him hell no. Rudy told her forewarned was forearmed. He kissed her, then kissed her belly and tried to undo her pants. She said no, that she hadn't showered in a couple days. They slept in a crawlspace.

He waited until the next weekend to email her: blackcass79@ hotmail.com, said her scribble on the back of the flyer. Hey you, she replied, I didn't know if I'd hear from you. He came to visit, fourteen hours on Greyhound from Gainesville. She had a fresh art school degree and not much else, so she packed a duffel and joined him on the return bus. They sat on the back bench in the cloud of formaldehyde and ammonia. In a tribute to the enveloping power of lust, they slipped into the bathroom; then, a few minutes later, lay down with their bags for pillows, and let the bus bump and tumble them to sleep.

JULES CHANCE CAME from Athens, where he'd soaked up all the old rock lies. Where you could be a rock star but you could also be a neighbor, and both seemed equally plausible. "You know what they say," he said. "In Athens you don't lose your girlfriend, you just lose your turn." He'd filled up his punch card and gotten out ahead of his reputation. Atlanta was too close: that's where all the Athens expats went. He kept his blond hair cut conservatively short except for an insouciant pouf in the front. He wore inoffensive tortoiseshell glasses. He had the former prep-school boy's distinctive ability to wear a blue button-down shirt and still look disheveled (untucked, skateboard).

Cass and Rudy rented a dowdy ranch house at the end of a cul-de-sac, on Northeast Tenth Place by Northeast Tenth Street, or was it Northeast Tenth Terrace, cross street Northeast Tenth Avenue? Chain-link around the yard, neighbors with a tent over their car and a tarp over their Jet Ski, everyone's house shrinking into that creeping Florida mix of trees, vines, and weeds.

They had a long bed with pillows at both ends. They'd built the frame out of spare plywood and scavenged two-by-fours. Not a masterpiece of craft, but form followed function. The heavy quilts were sewn roughly with thick thread. Rudy had never liked sleeping under a lot of blankets, but she'd inherited some and he'd gotten used to it. They'd read to each other—he from paperback classics, Shakespeare and Moliere and whatever else he scavenged from semester's-end sidewalks around the university, his patchwork attempt to rectify the embarrassment of his collegiate implosion; she tracts and manifestos from the infoshop where she volunteered—and challenge each other to games of quotation and aphorism until they tired or the light died. Lying on their sides, her soles on his shins, she'd reach back and grab his hand, wrap it across her torso to hold her breast, sigh and fall asleep.

They lasted a month on their combined half-salaries, then put tag-fringed flyers on telephone poles on University and the health food store corkboard. Jules moved in with his guitar, and more clothes than they expected.

And through Jules they met Seb, who had arrived on a bus from Philadelphia and wooed every guitar player he could track down before finally cajoling a skeptical Jules into a tentative partnership. When he found out that Jules's new roommates could pass for a rhythm section (Cass had played in drum corps in high school, and Rudy at least owned a bass), he turned the spotlight of his considerable charm on them. If Jules was persuaded by him, Rudy was seduced.

His real name was Sebastian Pomanth, so he went by Seb. He peddled an intoxicating ideology, or simply an ideology of intoxication. His encompassing passion for punk rock, and the strict ethical (if not moral) code he associated with it, rather ennobled punk rock than diminished him, but it limited him too. Teenage refuseniks make art by accident.

He was scabrous and verbose, with an acid-brass voice, and smirk lines on his left cheek—like laugh lines, but less ingenuous, the calcification of a short life spent at odds with the world. He had a kind of stiff pompadour, and wore a bomber jacket over a tank top tucked into high-belted pants. He liked, when they were at the bar, to whip a comb out of his inside breast pocket, dip it in his Jameson's, and run it through his hair. He'd tied a leather thong around his waist a few years earlier and intended to leave it on, maybe, forever, to ensure he wouldn't slip into a beery pudge like everyone else: a check, his teen self reaching up through the years to rein him in, a corset and a censor. Seb thought of adolescence as a kind of foresight, that youthful concerns were the same as those of a mature poet—truth, honor, the nature of identity— and that the young expressed them with more purity. Adolescence was boring, Rudy thought: It's the only time we take things seriously. Adolescence was crucial, Seb thought: It's the only time we take things seriously. "I want to live my life in the first-person spectacular," he told Rudy. Seriously.

He must have thought that was a good one, because it was the first line of the first song they wrote together.

"THANK Y'ALL FOR coming out early!" said Seb. A handful of people huddled by the bar walls and support beams. "I knew it would be worth it, but you didn't. Congratulations. You made a good choice. Maybe the only one either of us will make tonight. We're Expatriate Games, this one's called 'There's No Government Like No Government!'"

"Fucking hell," said Jules later, in the back room. He buttoned his sweaty shirt around a wire hanger, pulled the shoulder seams straight. "There was nobody there."

Seb was still electrified and pacing. He jumped on the couch, jumped back down. "Ah, fuck off. This is showbiz, Jules. They can like me—us!—or not. I'm trying to tell them things. Not to mention show them a good time."

"Showbiz! Small fuckin' taters. We sucked."

Rudy sat, knees together, in a soiled wingback chair in the corner. He hugged the body of his bass against his chest, deep-breathing the anxiety and exhilaration. "I don't think we sucked," he murmured.

"So fucking what if we did suck," said Seb. "The number one experience of being a musician is people thinking you suck. *Telling* you you suck! When you're new, they want you to shut the fuck up so they can eat in peace, or so they can see who they came to see. When you're coming up, they say you suck 'cause of competition, and everyone's suspicious of the new shit. When you're a big deal, they *really* say you suck, 'cause everyone wants to talk shit on the big dogs. Then eventually they say you're washed up and you'll never be as good as your old shit. That's the whole deal: people telling you you're amazing, which you already think, so it doesn't do any good; and people saying you're a piece of shit—which you already think too, but who wants to be reminded."

He struck an oratorial pose, realizing he'd been ranting. "Oyez! The vodka is speaking in me!"

"Sample the ham," said Jules, without malice.

Seb, not offended, cracked open a grin. "My heroes have always been laughingstocks. Now come on, there's gotta be some-one here who can show us a bad time."

5

THE BARS THEY liked then were the same bars Rudy liked later, but louder. Rudy and Cass and Jules and Seb went to the Hara-Kiri Lounge twice a week after rehearsal. Couple of other days, too. Rehearsal itself was only partially about practicing. They started cross-legged on the stained rug, or squatting on combo amps, with a magnum of red, a couple six-packs, and wine-bloody plastic cups. The songs mostly grew out of intense forehead-to-forehead sessions between Rudy and Seb. Rudy wasn't the musician Jules was, but his devotion to Seb was deeper; plus he had the patience and the fierce standards to challenge Seb and force him past glib first thoughts. More than once, he offered such comprehensive edits to Seb's lyrics that Seb just said, fuck it, you sing that one. You broke it, you pretentious motherfucker, you bought it. With the band, they'd run a new song, stop, fight, run it again. Get it through everyone's this-sucks filter, hack at it, file it down, rebuild it, retire to the bar.

The Hara-Kiri: unmopped black-and-white tile floor, pressed-tin ceiling, tarnished mirror, taped-up Polaroids and onion-skin newspaper clippings behind the bottles. Three taps and Popov in the well. None of that light beers five for ten bucks, bucket of brews, tray of shots: keep the college football crowd out. Cash only.

Seb's nihilistic charisma was thrilling, and infused Rudy with the feeling of belonging to a cadre that was both egalitarian and, since its ideology flowed from Seb alone, a benign autocracy. And Seb offered practical commandments to live by, an off-the-rack code of conduct for the blank spaces in their personalities: *No sunglasses on stage. Bring your sleeping bag; not a pillow, that's what your jacket is for. Use your last twenty to buy a round of drinks before you buy dinner for yourself. No rules but our rules.*

But Seb had more to show him than a canon of etiquette and aesthetics. The first time Rudy went to the Hara-Kiri with Seb, someone went around the table collecting twenties—for "stuff," they said. Rudy threw a bill in, to be collegial. A different someone came back twenty minutes later and dropped a little white packet on the foil of Rudy's eggplant parm hero. Rudy picked it up by a corner and studied it. He leaned over to Seb. "What's this?" he asked.

"Toots, ya rube. What'd you think we were getting?"

"Weed, I guess."

"Well, I'll take it off your hands if you don't want it."

"Nah." Rudy took another look at the bag. "I'll hang onto it."

"None must, all may, some should," said Seb.

A few weeks later, once he'd gotten the idea, Rudy went with them on the run. Powder's—how they got away with that!—was a few blocks away. Corner bar with no windows, black door with a flap, a knock-and-peek situation. Rudy expected this kind of place to be dank, but it was sharp fluorescent, karaoke on Fridays, a plastic palm tree in the corner, order a Corona from the bartender for show, sit a minute at the bar before you go to the other room. Stand casually by the DJ booth with your twenties. Hand comes out of a square knee-height hole in the wall, replaces the cash with a few baggies. If you're in a hurry, there's a sniffing booth in the

back corner, a black-painted closet with a velvet cloth instead of
a door, shelves at a variety of convenient heights. Somebody in
there already—nod politely. Meet some nice people that way.
This is the shittiest ever, one professional-looking man told him
happily. I can do a bunch and go straight to bed. Feel like I'm still
in the game. New wrinkle, try it from that divot between the
tendons at the base of your thumb. You know what that's called?
The anatomical snuffbox. Yeah, people been knowing that trick
forever. Chalky drip at the back of the throat, numb gums. Shame
the bathroom at the Hara-Kiri was so nasty, since half the stuff
was baby laxative. It got so just the smell of paper money or the
jingle of keys made Rudy's guts cramp.

Anyway, the point wasn't the stuff, the point was to have more
gin and tonics. The bartenders chased them out of the bathrooms,
banging and yelling; *almost done, shit, fucking calm down. Aren't I*
buying enough drinks? Sorry, fuck, I'll clean that up, gimme another.
I said I'll clean it up!

They amused themselves by harassing minor rockers who'd
come through on tour and wanted to go out for a nightcap, get
some local flavor, give Cass the old I-can-take-you-away-from-all-
this routine. (Harassing, but also flattering them, out of a kind of
belief in the alchemical power of proximity to even small fame.)
Hey man, yeah, I can get some stuff, I can hook you up. Gimme your
phone number. We'll go out for sushi sometime.

But by then the band was up and running: the Expats, as
people around town were starting to call them. From conspir-
ators fueled by alcohol and sexual novelty to partners in a fledgling, endangered business enterprise: "Many," said Seb, "are the
resources of courage and poverty." Shows booked. Vans rented—
"Don't rent a car with someone you haven't slept with," the
counter guy advised Jules. "Where there's a rule, there's usually a

story," said Seb. Maps bought and fought over. The long search for pay phones in unfamiliar cities when they got lost. ("The state bird of Florida is a busted white dude with a medical-grade sunburn walking on the side of the highway," said Seb, who didn't drive, from the passenger side.) *The sudden wild thunderstorms of the South, awesome and impressive,* read Rudy aloud from the back seat, without looking up from his book, as they drove through one. Cass, asleep with her head in his lap, muttered and pulled a thin black shawl over her face.

"Shut the fuck up," said Jules jovially. "What are you doing back there?"

"Reading, what should I be doing?"

"Drinking, man!"

The confinement, but also the excitement, of the van: the hothouse quarters, the hours available to sharpen and rehearse their repartee and their rapport. The empty bottles that began their rumbling circuits of the wheel well as they pulled away in the mornings from whatever ranch house's floors they'd slept on. The rehashing of the night before, the recriminations, the ridicule. The battle over cassettes, over radio stations, over sing-alongs, over silence. The scent of sodden rot from the sweaty show clothes crumpled in the back, or laid out over amps to bake in the greenhouse sun. The curled-up catnaps fueled by musty valerian stink-pills. The thrift-store and filling-station junk bought on impulse, then thrown on the dashboard with the curling atlases. The maps missing the one page they needed. The books shared, then ground underfoot. The greasy, crumby Mylar junk food bags shoved under seats. The duct-taped mirrors. The friends and hangers-on perched on suitcases next to seats; or knees-to-chest, backwards on the floor between the driver and shotgun seats. The clockwork bathroom stops. The mystery pills, gifts or barter, that gave them sore throats and made it hard to pee. The bottles and boots and bodies that spilled out the side door onto the gas-station macadam. Shards of glass, shards of light. If anywhere was the heart of their friendship, its novelty, camaraderie, wit and ingenuity, it was those bench seats.

They began to expand their range: the football wastelands of Jacksonville, the insipid crud of Tallahassee. Two to a motel bed when they had to; tape down the hair dryer trigger for white noise and bathroom privacy; shower cap over the smoke detector for the cigs and joints. Valdosta, Pensacola; the amoral miasma of New Orleans, where when you were ready, it seemed, you could just dissolve into the booze and heat. Pale with multiple-front hangovers, they pulled into an unfranchised gas station—next to a graveyard, with a bar attached—in the weird alien panhandle. A bone-thin creep in a squalid tank top dismounted his truck and gave them a look.

"Uh-huh," he said. "Yeah, I used to be in a band. What's the name of this faggot outfit? The Expats?" He sniffed. "Good luck with that." He returned from the store with a dangling six-pack of Heineken cans, decanted one into a plastic travel mug, set it in the cup-holder, and drove off.

They rented a rehearsal space in a bankrupt office park. It still held a few disconnected phones, and a backless rolling chair, and there was a little unraised porch from which they could sit out front and watch the rain march down the street. Rudy had never seen that anywhere else: a sharp edge to a shower, a straight line of water briskly swallowing the pavement.

6

"NADER?" SAID RUDY. He nodded toward a small green pin on Cass's thrift-store Pan Am bag.

"Yeah," she said, sliding into the booth next to him. The band practiced Tuesdays and Thursdays, but they still ate dinner together every Wednesday. "They had a table up by campus. They're trying to get him here for a rally. I think I'm going to volunteer. You should come."

Rudy attempted a combination of shrug, smile, and snort that he hoped would express support to Cass and sarcastic dismissal to Seb, without committing to either.

"Fuck him and fuck them all," said Seb automatically. "Voting just makes you look stupid."

"You don't need any help with that," Cass said.

"Seriously," said Seb. "So you work for this schlub. You knock on a bunch of doors and get harassed by idiots who will never agree with you. He loses, because he's a pedant that only white people and college students like. Then what? Seeing a bumper sticker for a losing candidate, even the day after an election, is like looking at porn after you already came. Gross. Sad, disgusting, you can't imagine even seconds later what it was that was so fascinating, you just want to forget about it."

"Grow up." Cass reached for a menu. "You think you're an anarchist, but you're just a cynic and lazy. I vote in all the local elections, the primaries they don't even want you to know about. My dad used to take me and let me flick the switches and pull the big lever. I still feel like there's something magic about it."

Seb unleashed a weaponized smirk. "Yeah, your dad's elections always went great."

That earned him a kick under the table. Cass's father was a member of the county board of supervisors back home in Pennsylvania, with two unsuccessful runs for statewide office to his name. His best result had been third in a Democratic primary for a state House seat. "You have a choice, but it's gotta be a meaningful choice. Gore and Bush, they're the same thing, they're bought and sold by the international corporations, the WTO, the IMF, all that shit. Look what happened in Seattle. Clinton sold out the Democrats. What's the difference between the politics of old Bush and now, other than that we want to kill different people today? We need a real third party. We just need to get the Greens five percent and they'll get federal funding in 2004, then we go from there. It's a process."

"All those old hippies in California and Oregon, though," Rudy offered, tentative. "If they go Nader, Bush could take the whole west coast."

"So what if Bush wins?" Cass said, heated now. "That'll teach the Democrats not to take us for granted. And it's not like it'll be a disaster. If you want to vote for a conservative religious corporatist, why not just vote for the real article? My guy wants government health care, he wants fair trade, he wants no more death penalty, he wants to break up the multinational corporations that think they're above the law. Don't you want those things?"

"I want my eggplant parm," said Seb, turning to look at the swinging kitchen doors.

"I mean, *what kind of country do you want to live in?*"

Seb furled back and looked directly at her. "I want to have nothing to do with any of those people, who are all monsters fueled by greed and ego. I want to not live in any place that thinks it's something that other places are not. I want to not live in a country, at all, if I can help it. I don't want that false name to be something that attaches itself to me or makes anyone think anything about me. I don't want it to be something I have to answer for. I don't want it to make me think anything about myself."

"Jesus Christ. Good luck finding your little patch of land floating in the void."

"A country can be a choice. A family can be a choice. A bar is a country, with natives, laws, customs, a dictator, even a border patrol. A band has a culture, a suspicion of outsiders, a dialect. What are we around this table, if not an entity—call it what you want—that looks after each other and understands each other?"

"Yes, the air is full of mutual appreciation right now," said Rudy.

"Who said family is all about understanding?" said Cass. "A family is people you are thrown together with and you have to work to understand, not people you choose because you fit together. Same with a country—you're born alongside all these other people, and you have in common something about the way you talk and the way you think and the assumptions you share. You can't just walk away."

"Can't I?" Seb tried to stand up, but caught his thigh under the table edge and swore.

"I bet anywhere in the world you go, no matter how long you live there, they'll always think of you as 'the American.' And you can never speak to your dad again if you want, but when he dies, you'll still be responsible for his debts." Cass turned to Rudy, who was fiddling with the plastic stand that held the beer list.

"Clowns to the left of me, jokers to the right," Rudy said, trapped by her expectant stare. "The most trenchant political commentary on the radio, available in every pizza shop and shopping mall in our capitalist world."

"Always a joke with you, Rude." She grunted explosively. "I know you're just performing for him"—the back of her hand to Seb. "A couple of opt-outers, one thinks he's too smart, one can't just stop being a grouch for half a second. Don't act like you don't care, like nothing moves you. I see you on stage."

"Give 'em the old"—Seb spread his arms and shook stiff-fingered hands—"razzle dazzle!"

"Bullshit," said Cass. "You believe it all. You're too good at sloganeering. If you didn't believe in it, you'd be in advertising; but instead, you're a singer in a punk band."

"What am I supposed to do," said Rudy, "join an underground cell devoted to the overthrow of the government? Revolutions are bloody and traumatic and people die and lose everything and have to move to new countries and start over as house cleaners and cabdrivers. How about an investment? Call my broker, the revolution's coming, I wanna go long on balaclavas. Yes, I'll hold."

"Asshole. I'll see you at home." She grabbed the Pan Am bag and threw herself out of the booth.

"An underground cell," said Seb with irony, or enthusiasm, or ironic enthusiasm. "Now you're talking sense."

"We can't even start band practice on time," said Rudy.

"From each according to his ability," said Seb. "Punk rock may be obsolete and simplistic, but it happens to be the tool we have to hand." He raised his drink. "To my first and finest disciple!"

...

Cass let the screen door bounce against the frame. A bird feeder lazed clockwise behind her. The neighbor's dog barked once, experi-

mentally, to establish the concept, then in a sharp conclusive string, rou-rou-rou-rou, to empty the thought. A crumpled White Castle bag lay toppled on the table, Sharpie scrawled in Jules's handwriting: "This seemed like a good idea. It wasn't. It was bullshit." His bedroom door was open. She knocked and leaned in, saw the neatly folded piles of pastel button-down shirts, the bare mattress the tone of a dog-spattered April snow bank. Jules was reckless with his person, but perversely finicky about his appearance. He'd spend a hundred bucks on a haircut or a pair of loafers or white pants and never get a fitted bed sheet. He was careful never to bring girls back here, anyway.

She closed the door and went to the room she shared with Rudy: mostly the plywood platform bed and a drafting table, which she'd insisted on, by the window. Something about its elegant expanse and angle could elevate a doodler, which is what she felt like at this point.

She sat cross-legged on the bed, then rocked forward, reached beneath, and pulled out her practice pad and sticks. Playing rudiments was as calming as playing the kit was cathartic. Single stroke roll: right left right left, dah dah dah dah. Water dripping from a gutter. Her arms had grown cables and wires. She had never been athletic—her jutting wide hipbones and nectarine chest and a pair of hammer-popped first metatarsals and all the other little asymmetries that had obsessed her as a young girl kept her from relaxing into her body in that kind of animal way—but the physicality of drumming pleased her. Like mopping the restaurant after closing, sweating in the sports bra she wore to work under her shirt, the tattoo of an alert rabbit exposed on her ribcage. She had always preferred to know, and be known, by touch. Talking was too . . . selective? Scattershot? Too precise: you diminished things by having to speak them out loud. Speech is silver. Why she liked Rudy, rude Rudy, who gave her own asocial urge cover by making her seem friendly by comparison. He wasn't the docile kind of quiet, but the sullen kind, unaffected by the awkwardness of silence. He could let a silence just sit there. Some-

times her own sense of social obligation couldn't take it and stepped in, which she resented—his abdication, her responsibility. But she understood: it was a game of chicken they'd both won.

Double stroke roll: right right left left, teeter totter, the sewing machine in full cry. Touch and sweat—the smell of the South was bloom and sweat and rot, the must that the decaying old shared with the resistant youth, those mutinous Bartlebys who preferred not to shower, preferred not to wash their stretch jeans and black band shirts. "I'm gonna blow the doors off," Seb would announce, as he ripped off his sleeves.

Paradiddle paradiddle: right left right right, left right left left, a brisk hopscotch. Flam accent, a tripping triplet. Damn, she's shredding bark, said Seb when he first saw her play. No tappers here. Why do girl drummers always have that wide stance, asked Jules. Why do guitar dudes act like they've got, like, powdered tiger penis around their neck, some kind of tribal amulet of virility, she threw back.

Ratamacue: right left right left right left, skipping down the road. Clocks tick in footsteps: the advancing lurch and the steadying grab. All of them came from comfortable homes. Seb's dad was a district attorney. Jules's was a backslapping, glass-clinking businessman, whose divorces hadn't materially affected his lifestyle. Rudy's ran a children's theatre. All of them basically liked their parents. All the punks did. Where did the anger come from, then? They were trying to tear down the comfort itself: the very love and success of their families gave them everything except a way to fulfill that very human, very American, need to overcome something. Everyone's narrative needs an antagonist. Why they played at poverty, the voluntary poor, catching themselves just short of actual hunger. The more squalid they could create themselves, the more they bragged it. Always time to tap out if it got too raw.

Triple stroke roll: right right right left left left, rifle fire. The alternative was to turn on yourself, and Cass had decided that was worse. Don't mourn, rage! Who is human and not angry! By the alchemy of feeling, to turn from sadness to anger wasn't necessarily an improvement, but at least then she wasn't tearing herself down, at least she had some agency. Identity was fluid. Those people who are the same as they once were, we call stunted. One of the surprising things about life was how many lives it turned out to be.

Buzz roll: here she comes, folks, Cass Loess, capital C capital L. She had cut her long, straight, dyed-black hair—it was getting in the way of her drumming now anyway—and discovered herself erotically inspired. A pinch of leftover masochism, a new slash of cruelty, a tenderness for this Rudy, this lean stolid boy with the voice, his long flannel sleeves and his unexpected formal locutions: Yes, I will do that for you. No, I cannot at this precise time, I'm sorry my love. The soft whistle of his passing lisp. His hair flapping over one eye as he bobbed, impassive, over his bass. His tawny crack, sprouting past his jeans. How his mouth went cold right before he came. If he seemed a misanthrope, she wished she could tell people, it was not from contempt, but abnegation. When he was a kid, he told her once, he would repeat his own words to himself in a whisper: a way of judging his own effect on others. Shaken by the results, he chose not to inflict, as he saw it, his unintentional rudeness, his involuntary offenses.

He didn't have Seb's serrated, garrulous charm. She hadn't told Rudy, probably wouldn't tell him, about the afternoon she brought a bag of grapefruits to Seb's house unannounced—vitamin C was good for that kind of boy—spent a few ambiguous hours as the audience for whom he blossomed. If nothing happened, it was because neither of them were willing to take responsibility for breaking Rudy. They had a code, after all. Sometimes she imagined Seb as one of those anima-

tronic life-size dolls, Lincoln, or Jack the Ripper, who sit motionless in a dark room until a viewer's entrance brings them to life. Call it narcissism if you like, but she felt a kind of generous power in being that witness who gave him his vitality. But he—Rudy—wasn't one of these young men who took unexpected flight after a new idea of who he might be struck him, and his firm Wisconsin substance was a dense, rooted hub.

She smacked a last accent, gathered her sticks clattering in one hand and wiped her eye with the other. Felt a sandy crunch in one duct and cleared it.

7

A SHOW DAY gleamed on the calendar. The anticipation was too pure to risk sullying, and the afterglow was to be savored, so they took off work the day of, and the day after: Cass from the restaurant, Jules from the call center, Rudy from his job as the white face of the burrito shop, Seb from whatever it was Seb did all day. They half-worked in the same way they'd half-attended college: a mindless shift job was a blessing. The last thing they wanted was to leave work tired, their brain used up. Mere jobs weren't worth that.

Rudy liked to walk the half-hour from his house to the Prosper: a coffee shop by day, all-ages venue by the occasional night. Seb and Cass would load the minivan they'd borrowed from her ex-boss (not that anarchist bookstores had "bosses") and meet him there. The way was flat. The low shallow houses played a losing game with the Spanish moss, palm, vines, and bamboo. The damp vital rot, the cycle of life in one smell. Right turn along the brackish water, bordered by half-drowned scrub, of the bricked-in canal before it degraded into a glum brook. Past the Queen Anne gables and Victorian heaps, the sweeping oaks. Right on the main drag: the hacienda-tinted county library, tan with maroon highlights, a hexagonal tower topped by a smaller cupola with an ambitious steeple. A few blocks down, the drug court; then the squat, blocky tower of the Holiday Inn, abrasive and domineering.

The Expats' first release was a brief disc, practically a demo, called *Rough Magic*: mostly Seb's jubilant harangues, but two of Rudy's more melodic melancholiads as well. Cass designed the cover art, a scratchboard silhouette of a bird flying over a barbed-wire fence: unsubtle, but, Seb said, understatement has no place in propaganda. It became an unofficial logo. Some fans had photocopied stickers, four to a page, and slapped them on stop signs and bus benches around the city center.

A small, faux-cobblestoned pedestrian plaza: at its center, between two benches, stood a stout pillar wrapped in advertising. Like the library, it was capped with a hexagonal onion dome and a skyward spire, a Morris column erected by some Francophile city commissioner with a pretense toward glamour. Embedded in the capital was a clock, hands stopped at noon, or midnight. The shaft was quilted with posters: A community theater adaptation of *A Star Is Born*. Students doing *Gypsy* at the performing arts center on campus. Get your tickets early for *A Christmas Carol* at the Hippodrome. Posters professionally pasted, or feebly framed with puckered Scotch tape, shedding and flaking like a birch, exposing long-gone faces, aged and torn.

On a tree, the old rind frays away and lets the raw new bark breathe. Here, the new growth was impatient.

There—just above eye level, curving away to the right: the woodcut migrant bird, his band's name, today's date. At the Prosper. All ages.

Rudy was overtaken by a small coathanger figure moving at a shambling run. Bowl-cut bangs left a stringy fringe across a vaseline-shiny forehead. His glasses were perfectly round, and too large. He wore a faded plaid flannel unbuttoned over a pristine white Expats bird-and-wire T-shirt. On the toes of his sneakers, he'd drawn, with gold marker, cat ears and whiskers.

"Rudy! Hey, you're Rudy from the Expats. Holy shit. I'm on my way to the show right now. *Rough Magic* is the best thing I've heard all year. Well, definitely in my top ten. . . . Oh, of course, man, you're welcome. I mean, you guessed that from the shirt. Ha ha, I'm that guy. Do you mind if I walk with you? I mean, I guess we're going to the same place. Hey, I just wanna say, and I'm not just saying this to you, but I love those two songs you sang. . . . No, really! I mean, I love Seb, obviously. His songs get me so pumped up and I just want to *yell* 'em and put 'em on a sticker and stick the sticker on my shirt and stick the shirt on a, like, a flag and wave it around while I'm yelling! But yours are, like . . . I can *feel* them, but I don't know if I could say what they're about, you know? I like that. Are *you* gonna do a record? I mean, *I'd* be interested. I'd buy it. Hey, I've got a four-track at my mom's, I got it at Goodwill, you could record some stuff there if you want. Holy shit, that'd be amazing! . . . Oh, right—Ryan. Ryan Orland. . . . Uh, fifteen. . . . Yeah, I know. Well, tonight's all ages, so it's cool."

Ryan paused, and the back of his neck turned bright red. "Hey, can I give you something?"

"Yeah, of course, man," said Rudy. The unfamiliar adulation made him magnanimous.

"I don't know if you're interested. I mean, I'm sure you're not interested." He pulled a cassette from his canvas army-surplus shoulder bag. The sleeve was hand-drawn and photocopied, roughly trimmed to fit the case. "Antonio Records, yeah, that's just me. Uh, when I was a kid that's what I wanted my mom to name my baby brother, but I never got one, and I never had a dog, so . . . I dunno. It's stupid. I hope you like it."

Rudy turned the tape over in his hand, looked at the back,

looked at the spine, looked at the blush that had spread to the kid's ears. His guileless admiration was both flattering and hard not to condescend to, just a little bit.

"Do you want to play a couple songs tonight?" Rudy said impulsively.

"What?"

"Before Culvert. You could get up for like fifteen minutes."

"Ho. Lee. Shit. That would be amazing! Are you serious?"

"Why not?"

"Ah . . . eye . . . yah . . . I don't have my guitar with me."

"So go get it. I'll talk to the sound guy. You can plug into Jules's amp."

"Holy crap. OK. I gotta run home. Thank you *so* much. I can't believe this."

The kid turned and ran, the flat soles of his sneakers slapping against the asphalt and the tail of his flannel flapping behind him. His bag, slung too low, buffeted his thigh, until, without stopping, he reached down and tucked it up under his arm.

RUDY ARRIVED, HE thought, first. The Prosper was the middle unit of a three-storefront brick building. It had a yellow marquee illuminated by hanging white lily-of-the-valley lights. A short blackboard tented on the sidewalk out front, until a gust of wind folded it smacking to the ground. Rudy flicked it back open, stood it up. "Green Party Benefit," it read in pink chalk. "The Expats." In smaller blue letters, below: "Culvert (ATL)." Smaller still, yellow, across the bottom: "10 p.m. doors. $5 suggested donation."

The two front windows, and swinging door, were near-obscured by black-and-white flyers and neon beer logos. The neighbors were a business-hours nail salon and tattoo parlor, so when the Prosper slipped imperceptibly from acoustic singer-songwriter

Thursdays to bands on weekends to live music six nights a week, complaints were minimal. After the coffee shop closed around seven, the tables and chairs were moved to a back room, exposing the gritty tiled floor left over from its original incarnation as a pizza parlor. At the back of the main room was a short stage, raised a foot above the floor and covered with stained, duct-taped, and stapled-down carpet. The ceiling trim was enlivened by a single string of neon rope. A lumpy ceramic soapdish with hobbyist glaze sat on a ledge behind the skeletal drum kit. Over it, a handwritten sign encouraged, "Take A Pick/Leave A Pick." Smiley face.

A side room lined with vinyl booths served as an ad-hoc arena for merchandising, music-escaping, bag-stashing, liquor-sneaking, scene-beefing, score-settling, peacocking, and order-pecking. In the back of the room was a booth that the Expats had claimed as their receiving area. Cal, the manager of the Prosper, left a few bottles of wine and gave them tacit permission to augment that at their discretion.

Jules was already there, alone, his guitar stretched out atop its case awaiting fresh strings. He was shuffling a little dance and singing to himself, a cheerleader's refrain: "I feel worse"—*clap, clap, clap*—"when I don't drink"—*clap, clap, clap*—"what's that called?"—*clap, clap, clap*—"what's that called?" He chuckled and took a sip from his cup, already fibrous with white crumple marks. He reached his chorus: "Red wine, white wine, any kind of wine!"

He sucked back the dregs and raised his hands in solitary triumph. A stray drop wriggled past the lip of the cup. It landed on the shoulder of his yellow oxford shirt and wicked outward. "Shitting fuck!"

"Hey Jule," said Rudy. "What's good?"

Jules twitched left. "Oh hey, Roodge. Just ruining another shirt before I even get onstage."

"Out, damned spot, huh?"

"The human stain. They usually come out in the end. If not, fuck it, there's always other shirts. Why weren't you at the space for load-out?"

"Wanted to walk."

"Bass players load the van, man, that's the rule. Everybody knows that."

Rudy laughed. "Oh, hey Jules, there's a kid who's gonna play a few songs first of three. I told him he could use your amp, hope that's cool."

Shrug. "Guess so. How much damage can one guy do."

"Hey, you scumbags," Seb announced from the door. "Van's out back. Come grab your shit."

"Can't park there," said Jules.

"Think globally, act locally," said Seb. "All I ever wanted from anarchy was to park anywhere and drink in public."

THEY CAME IN pairs and threes and gangs, the whole familiar crew: Mayfly and Squirt, Kodak and Caliber, Cattywumpus, Jimmy Locust, Metalhead Steve, Top Shelf and Al, Big Job, Pirate Jill and Jack Lemon-Lime. (The power move was no nickname at all.) Flirting and fighting and flattering, stealing drinks and sharing drugs, picking up conversations where they'd been left off last show or last month or last year. Who's missing? Who couldn't make it? Who's new that everyone already knows? Who's been excommunicated? A couple people said the guy in the top hat was being a creep. Keep an eye on him. Fuckin' kick him in the nuts if he tries anything. That girl with the white streak in her hair was getting drunk and making a nuisance of herself at parties. Yeah, but still, she was fun. Lucas went back to school, said he'd be back over break. Danielle broke up with her boyfriend and he was the one who was bringing her to shows, so she probably won't be around anymore. Meanwhile her buddy Margo, who everybody called Mango because it was funny, it was like she was trying to get on every guy on the scene, which, whatever, you know, guys do it, girls do it, even educated—well, anyway, it was fine, but come on, fucking give it a rest for a minute, right? And Jimmy Locust and Top Shelf were getting a band together, or had gotten a band together, or they had recorded a rehearsal, anyway they were gonna try and get Seb a copy of the tape and maybe open one of these Expats shows. That'd be cool. Anyway, check out this sick shred sled I just got.

The ambient clamor was barely dented when the kid—*who's that? Feel like I've seen him at shows. Ryan?*—stepped uncertainly onstage and unzipped a new-looking gig bag. He retied the fat shoelace of a dirty sneaker. He pulled out a white Stratocaster knockoff with a red strap, and plugged it into Jules's amp. He flicked the power switch and squeal of feedback soured the room. He cringed an apology, tuned twanging and audible. I'm gonna have to let him know about in-line tuner pedals, Rudy thought.

He approached the mic, uncertain. "Hi, uh, I'm Ryan." He blinked through his clammy bangs. "I wanna thank Rudy from the Expats for letting me play tonight. This is super exciting."

A trebly cheer—*yay Ryan!*—went up from the stage-right corner: a dozen or so of his friends, rounded up for support and crowded around the riser.

"This is called 'I Can't Take Myself Anywhere.'" He stared at his hand on the neck of the guitar for a long second, then closed his eyes and began: a tenor with an ostentatious tremor, an elaborate but involuntary vibrato. His cheering section clapped along in encouragement. It wasn't just that they were his friends, Rudy thought—he could speak to them in a shared language that Rudy, even in his twenties, was already outside. Too green for metaphor, the songs were raw, but Ryan was writing them and singing them from within the feelings still, from his teenage immediacy.

"Hey," Seb nudged him. "It's tiny Rudy! Where'd you find this little buddy?"

"That's not what I look like."

"I mean, he sounds like you. He's even got your wobble."

"I think he's alright, actually."

"You would."

"Hey, thanks you guys," said Ryan to scattered applause from the room and concentrated yelps from his claque—and a few others. His full-moon glasses were fogged. "So, I don't have any records yet really, but I dubbed like a dozen cassettes at home"— he reached down and pulled one, with a blank paper sleeve, out of a plastic grocery bag at his feet, held it up—"and I'll draw something on the cover for anyone who wants one, OK? Just come say hi afterward. Uhhh . . . yeah! This one's called 'I Before We Except After She.'"

"Adorable," said Seb to Rudy. "You must be a proud papa. Meet me in back when you're done at the kids' table."

"WELCOME! THANK YOU for your continued support of the Good Old Cause," Seb announced in his asperous howl, and saluted. "Release me, with the help of your good hands." Pocka-pocka-pocka drum starter pistol shrapnel—and begin.

How did it feel for them, the explosive crash of cheers, the endorphin wave, the burn of overloaded eardrums? Not "euphoric." Not "like the music was speaking through them." Not "like something connected them to the audience, that was unspoken but visceral." Not "a communion." Not "raw, cathartic." Not "genuine, authentic." Not "transcendent."

But—yes, like family—or more. Like they shared a limbic system, like they were all body and no body, like early loves who aspire to meld, so they can be embodied in their bond. They could hate each other outside the moment, even right before the moment, but the alchemy of the moment blast-fused it into trinitite love. Like the blood that flowed through one flowed through all; like the impurities of the individual were filtered by the collective spleen, and the spleen and bile of each purified and dissolved in the adrenaline of the whole.

But—not that, either. Neither simple words nor corporeal metaphor was the medium: the medium was the moment itself, nothing more. The moment could survive for a while, an ebullient bubble above the trees, borrowing time before an unpredictable pop. The moment could diffuse slowly, borne away in bodies one by one like melting shards of light. The only certainty was its dissolution, the joy-death of the universe.

You could spend the rest of your life trying to stay in that moment. Trying to keep that moment alive.

But—they were also conscious, and calculating, and aware. Seb hit his marks, choreographed his spontaneity, delivered his scripted adlibs in a throat-shredded bark, delivered his songs in the bestial howl of preverbal nature. Jules, his hands autonomous, scanned the crowd for the kind of faces he liked—unprepossessing enough that they'd respond to the attention, smart enough to read his subtext, genially reckless or intrigued enough to say what the hell—made and held eye contact, opened his face to match their bright and shiny enthusiasm.

But—Rudy stared at Cass, her bare arms taut and shiny, the hair at her jawline curled in the humidity, eyes down, consumed in her pummeling work. He turned to his teetering microphone, spit the dysgeusic flavor from his lips, howled his thin, tremulous harmonies over the noise, swelled his cheeks with beer during a four-bar break, the spill running down his neck with the sweat, the bottle upset at his feet, foam flooding his cable and pedal.

The crowd split, formed a circle, linked arms over shoulders, conceived a ragged kickline. Someone's unlaced boot flew, gracelessly tumbling toe over heel, tongue flapping, up and through the drop ceiling. A cloud of dust and fiber wafted through the center of the circle, and a chunk of asbestos tile landed on the floor and split. The crowd cheered. Seb mimed what appeared to be lighting a cigarette off of, then tossing, a Molotov cocktail. Sensing the moment, he propelled himself up and forward off the center-stage monitor and grabbed the thin copper pipe that fed the sprinkler system. Swinging pendular, he punched and punched the ceiling panels, cracking and pulling them down, exposing wires and whitewashing the room in a fine chalky powder. He switched hands, apelike, and, as he swung his weight, the pipe began to pull away from its fittings. A thin jet of water saturated a farther corner of the ceiling. A pair of kids in bullet belts ran at Seb. They leapt and each grabbed one of his dangling legs. The entire precarious pipework buckled, and sprayed water hissing in every direction. As the crowd began to chant and spin in the swirls of muck, Rudy saw venue manager Cal through the mist, palms out and upraised, an expression more of shock and sadness—betrayal—than anger. Cass, responsible Cass, shoved her snare drum under one arm and ran to cram the merch into its duffel bag. Jules ripped off his unsalvageable shirt and wrapped it around his guitar. Seb lay on his back in the middle of the floor, awash in sludge, still yelling inaudible incitement now only to himself, his face a rictus of anarchic ecstasy.

RUDY STUCK A bottle of beer in one back jeans pocket and a bottle of water in the other. He thrust a hip into the fire door's push bar. The sudden silence of the alley exposed the piccolo squeal pulsing deep in his ears, which began to harmonize with a distant but approaching siren. He walked a few blocks to the plaza and sat on one of the benches facing the column. With an echoing pop, he pried open the beer. The cap skittered across the stones and disappeared under the facing bench.

The crowd would be chanting and marching, holding soggy ceiling tiles aloft as trophies, as the police pushed past. Jules would be calming howling Cal, blocking for Cass as she salvaged the essentials and snuck them to the van. Seb would have ascended to his apotheosis of chaos. Rudy just wanted to savor his ebbing shards of uncorrupted joy, which soothed even as they cut.

The plaza shimmered, now, in a full-moon fog. A rank of sodium cobra-head streetlights marched in file toward a vanishing point. A grainy halo of light diffused from the column, as the scarecrow spire shot a dark bolt of shadow leaping toward the sky.

RUDY SET THE screen door gently against the frame. The neighbor's dog whined, *rrrooouuu*, ruefully, as if chastising itself for the disturbance. The door was open, the house dark but for a glow from Jules's room. Rudy knocked softly and looked in.

There lay his friends, entwined on the bare mattress, in the flickering light of a candle: Cass half-propped upright, back against the wall, Jules in her lap, her right arm around his chest and her left hand in Seb's. Seb's eyes were closed and his head was on Jules's thigh. His right arm was swung back behind him, and his right hand held Jules's left. Jules, with his right hand, hugged Cass's forearm tighter to himself. Still in their humid clothes and boots, a pile of soft sleepy young animals. A battered Walkman on the floor played slow swing from its stippled speaker.

"Hey Rudy," said Cass tenderly. "We were wondering when you'd come home. C'mere."

Rudy took in their warm welcoming looks. He sat on the edge of the bed and took off his boots. He found a burrow between Jules's shoulder and Cass's arm. He pulled Seb's leather trenchcoat up over them all, and they closed their eyes and listened to the lush languid music until the battery slowed and died.

8

EVERYONE SUCCESSFUL IS a little bit ruthless, Rudy came to believe. Even simple art is a betrayal. You scavenge the words and actions of your friends and families, write their barely disguised secrets, borrow the bits of them that vivify your work. Then it's their choice to be aggrieved or to be a gracious co-owner. This was Seb's weakness: he was such a puritan, in his way, that he couldn't make even the smallest concession to self-interest—what he would have thought of as disloyalty—or to courtesy, or to business. His indolence protected his innocence.

Seb had been right about the mayhem at the Prosper, though: there were no consequences besides instant, useful infamy. Who're they gonna sue, Seb said. The band has no legal existence. Cal doesn't know my real name. Anyway, we didn't start it, the kids did, and he still wants them to come to shows there. The kids, for their part, will always side with us over even the most sympathetic promoters and managers—who, ultimately, are rule-makers and limit-setters. Ecstatic destruction is a kind of poetry, said Seb, and the kids can sense it. Like: this is just to say, I broke all the furniture in your house, which you valued so highly; forgive me, my arm felt so strong, and the sound was so sweet.

After their exile from the Prosper, at Jules's suggestion, they began hosting shows at the house—Expat House, as it became

colloquially known. Cass cooked gallons of plain pasta. Jules threw
a four-by-eight sheet of plywood over some overturned recycling
bins, called it a bar, and sold cans of beer and bottles of water for
cash. Rudy found a PA system, speakers on thin stilts—sound on
a stick—abandoned on a street corner by the college, and got two
of the channels working. Seb played host and master of ceremo-
nies, preaching his gospel of suave hedonism—*I would share my
wine with you, my dear, but I can't tell whether I love you or the wine
more, and I'd be jealous either way*—between sets by various friends:
Cataline, sure; Various Artists when they could get it together,
Culvert or Jenever or Lorem Ipsum when they came through
town; and, more and more often, Rudy himself.

"WELCOME TO MY comfort dungeon," said Ryan, descending the
wooden stairs. A tie-dyed tapestry shaded the window. A bare light
bulb set between floor joists was roughly painted purple, and only
the feathered ends of the brushstrokes around the screw thread let
some light brighten the bare insulation.

"No wonder you're so pale," Rudy said. "You got pet bats or
something?"

Ryan rooted around in a corner of the floor's dusty shag, found
a two-prong plug, and ducked behind a plush chair. A web of string
lights sprouted white around the room, a stellar array outlining
the framing and running up and down the support beams. Four
slumping couches defaced with duct tape formed a rough square
around a straight-backed wooden chair and a microphone stand. "I
keep it set up like this. I want to record when the moment strikes,
you know? Even if it's the middle of the night. Or if I'm on a binge,
like, it's all just coming, if it's always kind of dark down here I don't
even notice when the sun goes. I'll just crash out on a couch if I'm
tired and wake up when I'm not, it's all the same."

"Doesn't your mom make you come upstairs? Like, for meals?"

Ryan's solicitous grin broke, and his eyes seemed to settle on an irritant in the middle distance. "We're just . . . out of the habit of seeing each other," he said. "After we moved here, she was wait-ressing during the day and at nursing school at night; now she's at the hospital at weird hours. I haven't seen her for a couple days. Sometimes she leaves me some food by the door. Like a cat."

Rudy let the subject drop. "You're lucky you have a basement. I don't think I've ever seen one in Florida."

"The old owner was paranoid about storms. Joke's on him, the storms found him anyway—it floods down here every hurricane season. That's why it smells like a mangrove swamp."

"Be cooler if you could stand up straight."

"Yeah. He was only about five-two, didn't dig deeper than he had to."

Rudy lowered himself onto one of the couches. The support he expected failed, and he dropped, with a kind of vertigo, into the crack between the couch back and the slid-forward cushion; he folded into reclining, his knees level with his nose. He tried to get up, but only managed to shove the cushion farther forward, exposing the folded mattress. Rolling to one side, he scooted ass-first onto his knees on the carpet.

"Oh jeez, sorry," said Ryan, rushing to help him up. "Yeah, that one's kind of a junker. I shoulda warned you. Here, just sit in the hot seat." He yanked Rudy's forearm; when Rudy shook him off, he pulled the wooden chair back from the microphone like a maître d'. "We may as well get started."

Rudy had decided to take Ryan up on his offer to record, and they interred themselves in Ryan's oubliette. Rudy found struc-turally sound portions of the couches on which to curl up when he needed rest. Despite the soggy heat, he pulled a wool hat down over his face against the smell, his condensed breath clammy against his mouth. Ryan seemed not to require sunlight or fresh air, but work and Cass enforced Rudy's occasional emergence. For this he was grateful: not just for the chance to clear the mold from his sinuses, but to get a breather from obsessive Ryan, who could follow insistent retakes and overdubs with—when Rudy fatigued— compulsively repeated headphone listens to work they'd just completed. Sometimes Ryan would leave the tape running, and record himself opening and closing drawers of a rusty file cabinet, or knocking an exposed PVC pipe, or scraping a screwdriver across the corrugated steel that formed a rough fence around the sump pump in the corner.

Ryan had inherited his will and furious work ethic from his father, an army officer. His mother had tired, in Ryan's childhood, of moving from military base to military base, had taken Ryan and settled. He had trouble keeping track of where his father was posted, and his mother's long absences increased his sense of practical orphanage.

To Ryan, Rudy occupied a comfortable equilibrium between worldliness and accessibility—an older brother figure. Rudy enjoyed the feeling. They sat up—well, not nights, in their monurnal cave—talking, and Rudy let himself pontificate, advise: *If there's one thing I've learned about making stuff with words, it's this: always get up and write it down. You know how you're half asleep sometimes and you think of a great line, or you have a dream where you write something perfect, and you think, I'll remember this, but if I get up now I'll be awake for an hour. Same fallacy as when you wake up having to piss, not urgent, but enough. You don't want to wake up, but then you're just lying there half-awake half-having to piss. You won't remember it. Keep a pad by your bed and write it down. A quarter of the time it'll be illegible, another quarter it'll be meaningless, like some stoned epiphany, but the other half you'll have caught at least some shadow of it, Caedmon, you know, your unconscious mind in action, like Bigfoot, like Schrödinger's cat, like the dial between zero and one. Not saying it's all gold—lots of blurry Bigfoot pictures out there—but at least you caught it and you'll know one way or the other. It doesn't help you, of course, if you're trying to figure out what to do in your life, but sometimes, afterward, it helps you work out what the hell happened.*

Having Ryan as an audience helped Rudy express the romantic ideas about music and community that he sheltered from his friends, helped him release the catch in his spirit that sometimes restrained his generosity: *play for ten people like you're playing for a thousand,* he told Ryan. *And if you're ever lucky enough to play for a thousand, pick ten and play for them. Hell, if only one person shows, play them a few songs in the parking lot and let the sound guy go home early. These little utopias can barely be maintained for an hour, for a few months, so we have to respect them and take them seriously, they have to last us until the next incarnation of the great lost cause.*

"Do you mind if I show you something?" said Ryan. He opened the bottom drawer of the file cabinet and lifted out an armful of spiral notebooks and loose-leaf folders, shaggy with insertions and shedding scraps of torn binding, their covers shiny with rainbows and cartoon characters. "These are my songs. I just—I don't know which ones are good. I don't know how to know which ones are good."

"Jesus Christ," said Rudy. "There must be hundreds in here."

Ryan hesitated with a flare of embarrassment, then dropped the pile on a couch. The notebooks spilled and spread like strewn slabs of slate and sandstone. "I'm down here a lot," he said, unnecessarily.

"How many of these have you recorded?" Rudy picked up a notebook at random and flipped through it—pages scarified with blue ballpoint titles: "Hate Your Neighbor As Yourself." "A Ban on Liars and Dirty Faces."

"Some of them. Most of them." He couldn't resist: "What do you think?"

Rudy wasn't sure he wanted to offer an opinion. "You're writing from your journal, off the cuff, writing about yourself, and that's fine. But you need some of the stuff you don't understand right away. That's not so literal. Colorize your wounds."

"You mean cauterize."

"No, I don't." Rudy kept flipping, then stopped and handed the book to Ryan. "Hard to know from just lyrics, though. Can you play me one?"

Ryan tried to slap a bashful mask over his eagerness, but it didn't take. He grabbed Rudy's guitar. "I borrowed the chords from one of your songs for this one." He paused for a moment and looked up. "I hope you don't mind."

"Finders keepers," said Rudy. "All's fair."

Ryan, relieved, went to play; realized he didn't have a pick, patted his pockets, pulled out a quarter, strummed; stopped, frowned. Rudy handed him a pick. Ryan began again.

So this is our excuse for passion
So this is what remains of truth
There is no better cure than action
To return to you what once was blue

Everything once blue now turns to brown
Like leaves that fall and wither on the ground
I turned to you, but I couldn't make a sound
And everything once blue falls to the ground

He stopped. "That's not so literal."

"OK," said Rudy. "That's not bad. I like putting the lyrical hook as a tagline at the end of the verses, instead of in a repeating chorus. It's old-fashioned. And you get the advantage of all the associations of 'blue' without being hackneyed about 'feeling blue' or 'the blues' or whatever. In fact, you're implying that the 'blue' times were the good times, so that's a fun reversal." Ryan was almost purring under the praise. "But it doesn't make sense. Like, if the central image is about the natural withering of love—how many things, in nature, start out blue and dry up brown?"

Ryan started to respond, then hesitated. "Blueberries?"

"I mean, not really," said Rudy. "They get darker blue, then black. There's flowers—but the move from alive to not alive, color-wise, you're really talking green to brown."

"I'm not writing a biology textbook, I'm writing a song."

"I know, but it has to hold up to scrutiny. It can't just sound good."

"Plus green to brown, that's hacky, too."

"I know." Rudy grinned. "This stuff is tricky!"

Ryan strummed the open strings sullenly.

"Look," said Rudy gently. "Lemme play you something I wrote when I was fifteen." He took his guitar back. "How'd that fucking song go"—a churning rhythm of descending chords—"no, fuck"—slightly adjusted, higher up the neck—"something like

In sullen midnight parleys, I've become a requiem
For lazy summer hours spent all alive with strategems
For easy-caught, redoubt, bethought, flowers broken at the stems
In broken English I recite these thoughts
The rhymes that other anglers might have caught—"

He broke off. "I mean honestly, it's like a rhyming dictionary fucked the First Folio. And it rhymes thought with thought. Not that you can't get away with that, but it's, like, graduate level." He chuckled, and Ryan smiled a little. "I was showing off. But it's empty, it doesn't mean anything. If it's about anything, it's about itself—'look at me rhyming.' Your song, at least it's got a foundation of feeling."

He sat back, and leaned the guitar on a shredded armrest. Ryan relaxed, too. "Where'd you grow up, anyway?" he asked. "Like when you were my age."

"Wisconsin," said Rudy. "We were right outside Madison, but it felt like the sticks." He scratched his knee. "You're lucky, you know. You have access to cool. I didn't know. Seb gives me the remedial course, he says, so I don't embarrass myself; he means so I don't embarrass him. I just had the one or two corporate rock magazines and a CD store to tell me what was good. Leftover hippie mythologizing. I'd crack the longboxes and stick them to my bedrooms walls with blue-tack, like posters, lie on my bed and stare at them. Left blue stains all over the drywall paint. My dad was pissed."

"Not that lucky," said Ryan. "I have to live here. You guys chose this, moved in, made it the way you like. Colonized the place. Mom wants me to go to the university, save money by not leaving." He shivered convulsively. "I gotta get out of here."

"Let's get some fresh air."

"Not what I mean," said Ryan. "Anyway my mom'll be home by now."

"You don't want to—"

"No."

Rudy closed the notebook he was holding, and balanced it on the armrest. "Why don't we record one of your tunes, then," he said. "I'll work on it with you."

Ryan looked at him with gratitude and relief, and responded so quickly—"Let's start with '31 Favors'"—that Rudy realized this was what he'd been hoping for, even working toward, since they'd started. "I'll lay down the basic song, and then you can add to it." He slipped into the chair and picked up Rudy's guitar. *I remember when we were caught by the cops*, Ryan wailed.

> *Trapped like moths in the cold, cold light*
> *Running reckless like lunatics into the desperate night*
> *We took our shirts off and ran in the snow*
> *You and I and your girlfriend and the car and the radio*
> *We were buzzing and restless, ruthless and ready to go*

After a few hours—Rudy added some guitar, and a harmony vocal, to Ryan's specifications—Rudy had to excuse himself to go to Expats rehearsal.

"I really . . . ," said Ryan. "Thanks, Rudy. Thanks for helping me."

"Well, I think you're good," said Rudy. "I think I can help. If you think you need any." He began to pack up. "So when are you going to make a proper record?"

Ryan squirmed. "I don't know. I couldn't. I'm not ready. Not like you. You're the man, Rudy. I couldn't do this without you."

For the first time, Rudy felt a ripple of caution about Ryan's sycophancy. "I had a moment," he said, "when I was maybe a little older than you, where I made a conscious decision that my regrets, from that point, should be regrets of action, not regrets of inaction. I felt like I'd been too passive. Better to beg forgiveness than ask permission, right?"

Ryan nodded carefully, taking this on board.

"It's not like it'll be the only record you ever make in your life."

"You'll help?" Ryan asked. "You can leave your guitar here till tomorrow, by the way."

Rudy ducked under a flap of pink insulation hanging over the basement steps. "See you tomorrow."

HE BLINKED AWAY the blaring sunlight at the top of the stairs. A wiry, shrunken woman sat at the kitchen table, smoking, either indifferent or hostile to his emergence—not looking at him, in any case. The wide plastic frames of her glasses were yellowing; the lenses opaque, catching the glare.

"Hi, Mrs. Orland," Rudy said.

"That's his father's name," she said sourly. "You can call me Deborah. You two all done down there? I have a shift tonight."

"I can't speak for Ryan," he said. "I've got to be somewhere."

"Work, I hope," she said. She turned her head—tight, black astrakhan curls—and looked at him for the first time. "Aren't you a little old to be playing with him?"

Rudy hesitated. "I guess I would say we were working." When she didn't react, he added, "He's talented."

"Talented!" she said. "He's sleeping though school. I didn't bring him here to drop out and be a dishwasher who plays open mic nights."

It hadn't occurred to Rudy that there was somewhere else Ryan ought to be. "Music is a noble cause," he said, uncertainly.

"How old are you?" she asked.

"Twenty-four."

"Did you go to college?"

He didn't want to follow this line of questioning, but was, barely, too polite to just leave. "I didn't finish."

"And where do you work?"

"At the burrito shop on University," he said.

"Cook?"

"Counter."

She nodded. "Noble cause," she said. "Cooks feed people." She turned back to her cigarette, and the middle distance. "Maybe someday you'll be a cook."

AFTER A WEEK or so, Rudy realized that the energy of their sessions had subtly but definitively shifted, to recording the contents of Ryan's capacious notebooks—with Rudy's assistance, advice, encouragement, and input, but no longer his direction. He excused himself with a gift, a used book he'd scavenged—*it's called* Orlando Furioso—*what's that?—that's you*—took what they'd finished of his own material, and called the haphazard collection of songs, scraps, and sound effects *Flamed Amazement*.

Ryan, meanwhile, borrowed, or squeezed, or extorted, a few hundred dollars from his mother to fund a proper Expats record, recorded in the concrete bunker pay-by-the-hour studio downtown, instead of at Expats House like *Rough Magic*. Seb had refused, as a point of purity and unjustifiable expense, to consider pooling money for a real session, but—no, Ryan wanted to! He owed it to them! They, like, well, they knew how he felt about them. Look, he was writing all these songs now, man, just watching Rudy work, it gave him all these ideas; but you know, the Expats, well, you can't just record the band in my basement, can you? They called it *Export Me*, and Ryan threw himself into its promotion.

In his artless way, Ryan was becoming an entrepreneur. His messenger bag was always heavy with what he called his catalog. Antonio Records now consisted not just of the Expats record and Rudy's, but a cascade of Ryan's music, under names including his own. His songs were ingenuous, quavering howls of obsession, jealousy, and hyperliterate angst. His distance from both parents, and his long lonely hours, fostered his frantic drive and his aching need for community, for an extended, substitute family. He moved his mother's beige desktop computer downstairs and wrangled it, buzzing and chirping, onto the fledgling internet. He haunted messageboards and newsgroups, chat rooms and forums. He discussed, emoted, pontificated, shared, communed, evangelized—he expressed himself to anyone who would listen, honed his skills at enunciating himself in the words that eventually elbowed their way into the crammed, crowded stanzas of his songs, an extension of his urgent sucking want.

He would sit at a folding table for hours at the Prosper, at Expats House, at VA Hospital (the flaking mansion that housed a rotating membership of the Various Artists collective), talking up and talking about the music he loved, selling or giving away his albums, trading chapbooks, and *being among people* in what seemed to Rudy an incomprehensibly uncomplicated way. He wasn't a performer holding court—he was one among others.

Ryan, Rudy discovered, was a little shocked by Jules: he found Jules's womanizing distasteful. Jules was getting a reputation, Ryan said, and not in a good way. Those girls look up to him, he shouldn't be taking advantage of them like that. Rudy didn't know quite how to react to this—it seemed, to him, prudish. Wasn't this an acknowledged perk of being in a popular band? He put it down to Ryan's inexperience—people could get especially moralizing about sex when they weren't having it, when it seems even more intimidating and impossible. Like religious fundamentalists. Like Ryan's fascination with markers of childhood—the cartoons on his shoes and folders, the naive sketches on his zines and album covers, the sleepovers and nostalgic kids'-movie screenings he organized for his friends—it all smelled to Rudy like a desperate fantasy of prepubescent purity, of a time before the complications and brutality of adult sexuality.

Jules, for his part, distrusted Ryan. He's a little operator, Jules said. My dad was a salesman; I know how people like that work, keeping a mental account of what you've done for them, what they can do for you, giving you a little stroke when you need it, and a nudge. They don't even realize they're doing it, they just think of it as being sociable. But once you notice it—you can just feel yourself being managed.

Ryan passed into his late teens, and retained just an appealing residuum of his adolescence. His shirts now cosseted his slim chest. His bowl cut was grown out and trimmed into bangs. He'd broken his glasses at an Expats House show the year before. Seb, in the evil older brother tone he relished, took the opportunity to advise him: *Here's what you do. Get you that surgery, I don't know, call someone from a billboard, someone that offers installment plans. Yeah, but glasses aren't cheap either, right? You got three hundred bucks to spare now? I didn't think so. OK, so you give them their fifty bucks or whatever down, get your eyes fixed. Then just don't pay. Sure you can. All you gotta do is wait it out seven years and you're legally free. You're gonna be a musician, right? You'll be moving around, no fixed address, getting paid in cash. Nothing to garnish. Done.*

Terrible advice, but a lot of people took Seb's terrible advice.

RYAN TOOK TO the new social networks like a bee to green pasture. By the time he started taking buses to play in other provincial college towns, he had not just contacts but friends, friends he knew and who knew him intimately if not personally. He reached out, to people, to other musicians, to other enthusiasts; he sent fan letters, manifestos, queries, rants, condolences, encouragement. He made a business of it: made spreadsheets of all of his contacts, when they'd last been in touch, made sure not to let more than six months go by without dropping them a friendly message.

He was, in short, a man on the scene. A man *of* the scene: friendly, entrepreneurial, savvy, social in a way Rudy admired in direct proportion to how impossible that all felt for him. Ryan was a natural, sincere politician with, as they say, a grass-roots base who trusted him. It didn't take him long.

9

DESPITE HIS PARENTS' reflexive approval of most everything he tried, Rudy still found that he coveted it. His sister, Lauren, had gone directly from college to grad school in Boston. During her spring break, Charles and Olivia Pauver—who supported their son, but didn't entirely understand what he was up to, and wanted to meet his friends—flew with her to Florida to visit him. The parents gamely volunteered to stay at Expats House. The band, conveniently, had a show that weekend. Out of an anxious, imperfect courtesy, Rudy and Cass evacuated their bed (though they neglected to wash their one set of sheets) and made themselves a kind of pet pallet out of blankets on the living room floor. Jules chivalrously offered Lauren half of his mattress—he'd chaperone himself inside a sleeping bag—but she politely declined, and curled up on the couch. When Charles and Olivia, without judging or criticizing, moved to a hotel room the next morning, Rudy's embarrassment was small but real. His sister took over the bed.

CHARLES PAUVER WAS a large, gentle man from northern Maine, out of a line of French-Canadian loggers. His wife, Olivia, was petite and had attended an all-girls school in Buffalo. They met while on break from college, volunteering for a street-performance group that specialized in agitprop puppetry: each was responsible for a pole controlling the oversized papier-mâché left and right hands, respectively, of a twenty-foot effigy in a suit with a sign across his chest reading "Industrial War Machine." The simple choreography—the hands came together, ritually crushing a huddled cluster of Vietnamese children, then apart as the casualties (a single puppet, with a black drape) fell away, then together again, rubbing in a circular motion as if to cleanse themselves of responsibility—had the aphrodisiac effect of a courtly minuet. When, shortly, Rudy arrived, Charles found a job with a newly founded children's theater in Madison. Olivia eventually got certified to substitute at the elementary school. Two years later, Rudy's sister Lauren was born.

Charles and Olivia were hardly radicals. Their provincial upbringings were more traditional than conservative, but they were married, employed homeowners with two children by their midtwenties. Still, they identified with their times. Charles gently seasoned his fairy-tale productions with progressive emendations: a princess in pants, seven dwarves who organize the mine as a workers' collective. From time to time, he offered a Saturday morning drop-in seminar on set design in a borrowed university workshop. Olivia auditioned foster homes for the orphaned, free-floating presumptions of her Catholic instruction—tantra, homeopathy, Reiki, à la carte Eastern syncretisms (yes to the oneness of everything, no to the obliteration of self)—and eventually took up what she called "fiber arts." An experiment with homeschooling was overwhelming and brief, but they shared the firm belief that their children should be encouraged in their every interest—who knew what was a whim, and what a calling?

They would have described themselves as artistic, though their sensibility was limited by a stubborn denial of the spectrum, the complication, of human ethics. They were energized and hobbled by an idealism that required a willfully restricted moral imagination—peace, without the possibility of war; love, exclusive of hatred—an aspirationally childlike propaganda.

Their actual emotional lives remained mysterious to Rudy and Lauren—not that their parents wouldn't have explained themselves; they would, still, if only their children asked. Charles and Olivia believed that children should understand their parents not as distant and capricious authorities, but as people who cried, doubted, lusted, and—occasionally—regretted. They volunteered enough of themselves that Rudy and Lauren rarely found the appetite for more.

Parenting naturally trends toward conservatism: freedom means risk, wanting to keep children safe and secure means restricting their freedom, thus parents become enforcers of limitation. Charles and Olivia rejected this. We don't want them to be ashamed of themselves, they said. They should be able to explore their impulses. Rudy appreciated this, he supposed, but in their invitation to set his own standards, he found himself having to cobble together a personal code of behavior by an uncomfortable process of trial and error. He tried to reconcile, within his own personality, his mother's stubborn ideals with his father's increasingly ironic stoicism, or stoic irony, which managed to be both self-denying (Charles was a born talker) and solipsistic. Lauren, for her part, reacted by adopting a ruthless pragmatism premised on efficiency and no-nonsense conventional wisdom: she wouldn't be trying to reshape the world, thank you, it was enough to live in it.

CHARLES AND OLIVIA arrived early for the show. Rudy and Cass were out picking up the keg for their makeshift bar. The parents found two folding chairs in the garage and set them up with their backs against one of the side walls; not in the back of the room, but far enough from the stage that it wouldn't be, they hoped, too loud. They sat and read paperbacks (she a novel, he a biography of Mayakovsky) as the kids began to turn up, shoving and shouting, and the room began to warm and buzz. As the first band—Kayfabe, down from Tallahassee—started to make noise, they folded page corners and stashed the books under their chairs. After a few minutes, Olivia whispered something to Charles. He got up, disappeared for a few minutes, and returned with a handful of toilet paper. They rolled it into loose pellets and plugged their ears. Lauren took it upon herself to organize the merch table. Jules brought her a companionable drink, and they leaned against the wall and chatted while Kayfabe played. Rudy and Seb made a surreptitious Powder's run. Ryan knelt next to Charles and Olivia for much of the half hour it took the Expats to set up, talking and gesturing with enthusiasm, then listening attentively, with a finger pressed to his tragus. *Whynchu roll your tongue back in,* Cass said to Jules, nodding toward Lauren. *You don't eliminate the male gaze by mocking or dismissing it,* he said, flipping and plugging in his guitar, *you only drive it underground.* As Seb wrapped a loop of mic cable in his fist, Ryan pressed a CD into Olivia's hand, pointing out details on the front and back; then stood, gave them each a two-handed handshake, and ran to the side of the stage, where he began to bounce on the balls of his feet, his shoulder bag smacking against his hip.

IT WASN'T A particularly rowdy affair, as Expats shows went, but the end of the night got a little fuzzy, and Rudy didn't remember having said goodnight to his parents. (Ryan had. *You're so lucky,* he shouted in Rudy's ear at the Hara-Kiri later. *It's cool that your parents are so supportive. I don't think my mom's ever listened to my songs.*) Lauren had to shove him awake—he'd rolled off the makeshift mattress and curled up next to the couch—and remind him that Charles and Olivia were treating them to brunch. He pulled off his shirt and stuck his head under the bathroom faucet to wash off a layer of slimy, metallic sweat. With a clean shirt but matted hair, he could just about hold himself together until he got to throw a few forkfuls of home fries at his sour stomach.

"Very energetic," said his mother, over sweet potato pancakes. "You have some extremely enthusiastic fans."

"That's one word for it," said Lauren. "Can you pass the ketchup?"

"That boy, Ryan, feels very strongly about you," said Olivia. "He gave me the CD you made yourself. You didn't tell me you were making your own music!"

"I don't . . . " Rudy waved to the waitress, without looking at his mother, and asked for hot sauce. "I don't know if it's any good. It's just some stuff I'm trying to figure out."

"Well, I'm sure it's good. I can't wait to hear it. I always want to know what you're working on."

"It seems like you could charge a little more for your shows," said Charles. "Are you all making enough to live?"

"Five bucks is kind of the standard, Dad. Anyway, we're trying to build something. Putting the show money back into the band fund. I don't want to worry about the money for now. It'll come."

Olivia reached across the table and took his hand. "Talking to that Ryan," she said. "I did feel like what you all were doing was important. It sounds like he has a tough time of it at home. A boy like that needs people to look up to. I suppose he's not the only one."

A pause settled and exhaled.

"You're keeping yourself healthy, right?" asked his father.

"I guess so," said Rudy. "Enough. How do you mean?"

"You probably don't remember this," said Olivia. "You wouldn't, you were just one or two. What is the earliest thing you remember?"

"I have this vision of squatting over a stream in the backyard," said Rudy. "On a bridge, you know, two gray planks. In my overalls. Poking the water with a stick. And the glowing haze of the sun and the grass."

"That's a photo we have," said Lauren. "That's not a memory."

"Well, anyway," said Olivia. "You had a seizure, a febrile seizure. A fever that spiked. We were at a restaurant. I was having a flank steak. A treat, you know? We hadn't been out much since you were born. We knew you were a little sick, but we had planned the dinner, and, well, we figured you'd be OK. All of a sudden—we had just ordered a bottle of wine—your eyes rolled back, and you started convulsing, flopping around. I panicked—I just handed you to your father, like you deal with this, I don't know what to do. I don't know why, I'd always thought of myself as someone who could handle things, but in that moment . . . You remember?" She turned to his father, who nodded.

"Mom," said Rudy. "I've heard this story a million times."

"I cradled you," Charles said. "I said, Rudy, Rudy, come back. I thought I would cry. I told your mother to call an ambulance and she did. It's amazing how fast they were there—I found out later that they were just parked around the corner. But I didn't know that then. I was talking to you, calling you, and you were limp. I thought, this is how it happens—this is how I lose my child."

"Dad—" said Rudy.

"Let them tell it," said Lauren. It was a kind of recitation, a prayer of their love for their children, read from a shared, invisible breviary.

"It only lasted a minute or two, then you were passed out asleep on his shoulder," said his mother. "The medics said a seizure isn't really dangerous unless it lasts twenty or thirty. Can you imagine? *I* wouldn't survive that. They gave you Tylenol and saline. It was really nothing. But I'll never forget it. That's when we realized *how* we loved you. Your world is so upset by your first child, you know you love them, but you don't quite know the shape of it, or the depth of it, or how however much you think your life has been misshapen or broken or reassembled by them, it would be annihilated now if you lost them. Do you understand what I'm saying?"

Lauren was giving Rudy a look, so he said yes.

When he got home, he found they'd slipped under his pillow an envelope: five twenties, in a greeting card with an embossed red-and-silver heart.

10

NOBODY HAD BEEN surprised when Jules made a play for Rudy's sister when she came to visit, but everybody was surprised when she went for it. Even more surprised when he started flying to Boston to visit her. Jules saw her, Rudy figured, as the kind of person you fall in love with when you're falling for the third or fourth time—reliable, not too pretty, good with shopkeepers and landlords and aunts. What she saw in him was more mysterious.

"Why," Rudy finally sat her down and asked. "The guy's a scumbag."

"You're in a band with him," she said.

"Yeah, that's how I know."

"Look," she said, "first of all, there's a reason women like him. He's charming and he's good-looking. He can talk his way into and out of a lot of things. He's the kind of person people forgive. I'm no vestal here either. I can handle him and he can handle me. Maybe I just like taking in a stray dog."

"He's a drunk."

"So are you. So am I probably. Hell, who do we know that's not a drunk, I mean technically? There are worse things in the world than having a few drinks every day."

Export Me sold well enough—a few thousand copies, after some national distros picked it up—but Ryan's passionate advocacy of the band was more tolerated than embraced by his growing community of fans and friends, who were increasingly interested in Ryan's own music.

Meanwhile, Various Artists had a freakish breakout. Their kumbaya anthems to syndicalism and collective solidarity, it turned out, were unspecific enough to be indistinguishable from inspirational jingles; and they, it turned out, were politically flexible enough to license them. When "Power to the People (This Is Our Town)" leapt from sports-drink commercial to stadium anthem, the group (their membership had rapidly contracted and solidified) issued a statement listing the anti-capitalist causes to which they'd be donating the royalties. They'd be renovating VA Hospital, they said, bringing it up to code and applying for rezoning, so it could be a legitimate center for activism and all-ages shows. And—in keeping with the "support the scene" messaging— for their first big tour, they'd be taking as opening acts only their friends in other local bands. They hoped, they told Jules and Rudy privately, that the Expats would help them kick it off.

"Shit on that," howled Seb. "Bunch of fucking money-getters." Both his standards and his ambition were offended. "Think we're going to go on before those humbug hippies, those phony anarchists, that frat-party-under-commune-cover, forget it, I'll throw their fucking backstage cold cuts at them slice by slice and cherry by fucking tomato."

Energized by public outrage and private envy, he began agitating for the Expats—who had never tried more than ten days at a stretch, or traveled past the Southeast—to attempt their own national tour.

"That doesn't make sense," said Jules. "Why would I set ourselves up for failure, when we can play to a couple thousand people every night, with a band we already know?"

"Failure!" Seb rose to his feet, and to his occasion. "A band of gypsies, stealing to live—is that failure? A troupe of vaudevillians, singing for their supper—failure? A gang of pirates, rampaging across the country, comrades in arms? Failure!"

"Remind me what else pirates are famous for," said Cass. "It goes with pillage."

"I guess I don't understand what you're trying to prove," Jules said after a pause.

"I'm trying to prove that actions in life have a moral weight, that you can be an ignoble success"—Seb actually banged his fist on the table, twice, to punctuate the phrase—"just as easily as a noble failure"—bang, bang—"and if I'm going to play—if *we're* going to play for a couple thousand people, I want to get there the right way, the *noble* way, by gathering them to *us*, evangelizing, congregating, accumulating, one by agonizing one if we have to, because then we'll have *earned* their love and their trust and their affection, and having *earned* it we'll be able to, and deserve to, *keep* it. That's noble."

Rudy colored, inspired almost in spite of himself. "I can book it," he offered. "I'll make the calls."

"That's what I mean!" said Seb. "From each according to his long-distance plan. Ask Ryan to help you, he knows people everywhere. What about you two? Which side are you on? You have nothing to lose but your day job!"

Cass and Jules reluctantly acceded—no singer, no shows. But though Rudy did his best to organize a tour (Ryan, indeed, was happy to share his spreadsheet and suggest simpatico acts local to each town), he found their lives impossible to coordinate. Jules was spending more and more time with Lauren in Boston. Whether this was a form of passive protest was difficult to determine, but the band's schedule began to include more enforced downtime. Cass filled it with restaurant work and righteous causes; Seb filled it with lightly disguised pouting. Rudy realized how much more flexibly he could tour by himself, and used Ryan's contacts to take the idle van on meandering circuits of living rooms and coffee shops: nothing huge, but—*noble*, and enough to slowly accumulate his own name.

Eventually, local pride in Various Artists' success overtook any lingering qualms about their methods, and Seb's barroom tirades came to sound petty and passé. *Export Me*, and the idea of a long Expats tour, drifted farther into the past, and finally, imperceptibly, dissolved.

And that first big Various Artists tour featured special guest—no one was entirely surprised to read—Ryan Orland.

POWDER'S FINALLY GOT busted, and a week later, a limo pulled up in front of the Hara-Kiri. A window rolled down, just like the movies, you'd never believe it, a hand with a stack of business cards. We're Powder's, they said. Here's a phone number, you need anything, you call us. Rolled back up and drove away.

The Hara-Kiri closed not long after. The joke was, after all that, all those nuisance kids spending their fifteen minutes in the bathroom was the thing keeping the place afloat.

How do you even eulogize a bar? How do you eulogize a scene? The people they ruined disappear because they have nowhere else to go. The people who were just dabbling disappear because they do—and that was always the plan.

When Ryan called to ask Rudy if he'd come open for his—Ryan's—next tour, it didn't feel like years had passed: they'd just stopped seeing each other around town. Ryan would, he said, release Rudy's brand-new record *The Morris Column* on his own brand-new Bad Dream imprint. Rudy would get a little boost and, he thought, give Ryan a little reminder of which way the natural course of favors ran.

part III

11

"RYAN'S TAKING YOU out with him," Jules said to Rudy, over breakfast.

"Yeah. He's in a tour bus now since *Olifant* hit. He's not charging me for my bunk, it's like a nice gesture or something. Royal courtesy, the gift of snow and fruit."

"I mean, never hurts to have a famous friend."

"'Spose."

"Who else is playing?"

"Alessio Pashlo is gonna open, then me, then Ryan."

"Hoo boy. You ever seen old Less?"

"What's to know?"

"Used to front The Plural Nouns, now he's doing a solo thing." Jules paused. "I'm going to say something that sounds mean about someone I think is a really nice guy."

Musicians don't talk, Rudy thought, they talk shit.

"Or maybe I don't think that. Maybe I think he's just a special kind of idiot that once you start getting irritated by him you just can't stop. But he has this way of, every record he makes sounds like whoever his most famous friend is that year, and I guess it's Ryan's turn. It's no crime. I doubt he's anyone's favorite, but I bet he's a lot of people's second-favorite; like, if you like Ryan, Al's probably fine too. But he's the world's best opening act; he really works for it. His most popular songs are covers, you know?"

"YOU'RE RUDY? GREAT. I'm Pablo, TM." Tour manager. He frowned, a look somehow both domineering and put-upon. He dropped a cigarette butt and rasped it against the gravel of the parking lot. "Welcome aboard. Here's what you need to know. The door code is six-two-four-five. Lock that shit. We don't want randos wandering on board. Six-two-four-five-star opens the bays. There's a bunk for you, back bottom, across from the junk bunk. You been on a bus before? Leave your shoes in the front lounge. Sleep with your feet toward the driver, so you don't break your neck if he stops short. No solids in the toilet. I'll have a day sheet schedule and a sign-up for guest list posted in the front lounge every morning. Keep your friends away from backstage beer, we don't need any fuckin' rider spiders. Jackie is front-of-house, she's inside already, wringing it out. Cy's merch, Max is guitars and stage tech. If I had to guess, they're back in bed."

He flexed a humorless grin, and handed Rudy a laminated pass on a lanyard and stack of twenty-dollar bills.

"Here's your lammy and first week's PDs."

"PDs?"

"Per diems. Twenty bucks a day. I'll have them for you every Monday. You're two fifty a night, right? I'll pay you for the week every Monday too. Doors are at seven, show at eight, Al Pashlo's doing thirty minutes, fifteen minute changeover, then you'll do thirty, then Ryan does ninety and an encore. There'll be a merch table for you and Al to share. Our shirts are twenty-five bucks, so yours are too. Any questions? Good—no questions is my favorite thing."

The bus door puffed a hydraulic sigh and slid out and away. Rudy slipped the lanyard string through a side belt-loop, fed the laminate back between the strings and stuck it in his back pocket. He climbed aboard.

The driver's throne, steering wheel low and horizontal like a platter, was empty: he slept in a hotel room during the day. Rudy turned left and pushed through a split velveteen curtain.

IN THE FRONT of the bus, past the curtain, was a small lounge. When parked, the sides could be hydraulically extended. The windows were darkened to deter peepers, and had brown pleated window shades—drawn. To Rudy's right was a straight bench, with drawers beneath. To his left, a small molded table was bolted to the floor, hugged by booth seating. Past the table, a tall thin door— the bathroom—and past that, a heavy hatch that led to the bunks. The standardized design of tour buses must, Rudy figured, date to the seventies—certainly their interior design seemed to, heavy on wood paneling and chrome and industrial carpet. A scent of disin- fectant expired from the sloshing tank of urine underfoot.

Ryan stood facing the small sink basin. His cheeks were swollen and distended. He sawed at something resembling a desic- cated toe on a rough white cutting board, and stuffed a tan chunk behind his teeth.

He noticed Rudy watching him and spat what looked like bits of wood and sawdust into the sink. "Rudy! Welcome to Little Rock. It's great to see you. Pablo got you sorted?"

"Yeah, no problem. What's that you're eating?"

"Oh this"—he picked a hair from his lip—"I learned this from Alpha Serum when he took me out. Slices of raw ginger in your cheeks, like a lipful of K-bear. It's for your throat. Better than gargling salt water."

Rudy nodded. "It's good to see you, Ryan. Thanks for having me."

"Hey man, of course. It's been too long. And it makes sense with *The Morris Column* coming out. Did Rose from Bad Dream call you?"

"I don't have great service out here." Rudy offered his phone from a pants pocket by way of apology and demonstration.

"Shit, I bet not! What is that, one of those old Motorolas?"

Rudy protracted a telescoping antenna and unflipped the body. "I got this at a pawnshop before the first Expats tour. Still works. Basically."

"Telegraphs still work, but you only see them in museums. I'll tell her to call my phone instead. Press is good so far! I heard *Haystack* is gonna run a piece." Ryan detected a skeptical look, quickly suppressed, flitting across Rudy's face. "OK, whatever, look at Alpha, they made his career practically overnight. Synergy and shit. Anyway, I got faith, Rudy, things are gonna go off for you." He chewed a little, then switched his chaw of ginger to his other cheek.

"I'm impressed, Ry. Look at you. Bad Dream is a real thing."

"Well, yeah, you know, when I signed with Warners I wanted my own imprint. Antonio was, like, my CD-Rs and things, so I figured I needed a big new name for the big boy game. And after my record, you were the first person I thought of. You nailed it, man, the record is amazing. As usual. I can't wait for people to hear it."

"I appreciate that."

"These'll be good shows, too. Friendly people. It's like you told me once, there's no such thing as a crowd. It's each person with their reason for being there, and why they might want to go home early, and whether they need a drink, or their feet are tired, or there's a babysitter—well, not so much with these kids. I still think of that when I'm mid-song trying to decide what to play next. I pick a face and try to read what they need."

Rudy laughed. "I said a lot of things, Ryan. I'm glad that one worked for you. My performing philosophy now is a little more"—he paused and half-grinned—"autocratic."

"Which means?"

"I'll show you tonight."

"Alright, alright. Rudy can't fail." Ryan grabbed a denim jacket from the couch. "Come on inside, lemme introduce you to everyone.

"THERE'S A TRAVELING salesman," said Pashlo. The small theater was already full and chattering, the sound magnified by the varnished hardwood floor. From the wings, Rudy saw Al from behind, in three-quarter profile: jeans, clean plaid sleeves, piebald tattooed forearms, tight haircut secured with gleaming pomade. "He wakes from a nightmare in a hotel room. Grabs a book from the nightstand and throws it against the wall, then realizes it's the Gideon Bible. He picks it up, runs his finger down the page, stops at Revelations, chapter 10, verse 13, which says—and you're from Arkansas, so I know you know this—it says, 'No man stands so tall, as when he stoops to pick up a ukulele.'"

Rolling chuckles, scattered claps. The bustle of conversation by the back bar, under the low balcony.

Al was like a model home, Rudy thought, fabricated from the pages of an aspirational magazine, but with no wiring and no plumbing. Theoretical luxury, but when you looked closely the baseboard didn't meet the floor, the trim was pulling away at the corners, the wall sockets were misaligned, exposing the ragged edge of the wallboard. It wasn't cynicism—Al was sincere; cynicism doesn't sell, people can tell—but he was built hurriedly, and without craft.

"All right! Who's excited for Ryan Orland?"

A peal of enthusiasm, his if only by a transitive property. Puppyish bouncing from the front row early birds resting their crossed arms on the edge of the stage.

"I've got just one more song, thank you guys so much, check out Al Pashlo dot com, that's A-L P-A-S-H-L-O, and come say hi at the merch table later! This one's called 'Will-o'-the-Wisp.'"

Halfway through the song, Pashlo paused, playing quietly and rhythmically: the old I'm-gonna-need-you-to-help-me-out routine. He harvested claps, first from the front rows and then from the far corners. Kindergarten business: you do this, I'll do this; the gentle fascism and warm submission of crowds to power.

He finished the song with a rapid-fire strum and struck a pose, guitar neck held high. The marching rhythm from the crowd crested and crashed into a thermal pool of approval. As he knelt and unplugged and coiled cables, he accepted the congratulations of the front row with broad grins and nods.

The house music flattened the ambient noise into a clamorous alloy. Rudy picked up his case and walked up behind Al, who turned and rose.

"All yours, I warmed 'em up for ya," he said, shining.

Rudy saluted. "Nice to meet you, by the way."

"You too, boss. I'm gonna do some small-business work and then destroy some hummus and baby carrots. See ya on the bus."

A harried young man with a yellow cardigan—local monitors guy—pointed Rudy to a DI box. "Give me a strum and a yell and let's get after it."

"You got it," Rudy said. "Boss."

CHANG, CHANG, CHANG, CHANG. His guitar suddenly boomed through the PA, and the startled crowd slowly turned its collective attention to Rudy. "Hey hey hey HEY."

Generals of antiquity, he had read, were obsessed with fighting a battle on favorable grounds, and their armies would circle and shadow each other for days, even weeks, until the terrain was right. Rudy had come to feel the same way about audiences: there were some people he was never going to win over, and he'd rather drive them away so they wouldn't distract the ones he could. Set the conditions for a good show. Obedience prepared the tyranny of song.

"Hi there."

Hi, hi, offered sprinkled voices.

"My name is Rudy Pauver. We don't know each other, but you're stuck with me for the next thirty minutes. I'm not saying my words are more important than yours, but they're for sure going to be louder. So if that's going to mess with your good time, let me suggest the patio, or the foyer, or another fine drinking establishment in this fine drinking town."

A dozen or so people in the back of the room turned and left through the swinging doors to the front bar.

"Alright, now we understand each other." Rudy didn't yell, but his brusque confidence carried some authority—enough to buy him five minutes of attention. "With your grace, let me present you with this song about love and bad breath. Actually, if you're with someone who doesn't want to smell garlic on you, I'm gonna say you're with the wrong person. It's called 'Garlic and Vine.'"

> *The frayed shaft of the sun*
> *Makes the tower in the light jump into falsetto*
> *What do you consider fun?*
> *We can settle in the bandshell and play games with the echo*

You can hear the size of the big rooms, Rudy thought. Your voice comes back at you from the balcony in a majestic haze that gives you a little extra kick in the diaphragm. Makes you sing like a giant. Hypnotize yourself, if no one else.

I wanted to write you a short song
But I didn't have time
So I wrote you a long one
It made gods of garlic and vine

While his tongue and hands did their job, his mind roamed: *There's a draft from a vent across the ceiling. If only I'd brought one more beer on stage. Need more vocal in the monitor, so I don't have to swallow this mic, and Al's spit. The skinny fellow with the glasses and the brand-parody T-shirt—his kind only come the first year or two, when you're fresh meat. What song next? "The Billows Spoke," I guess; has a nice bounce to it. Over there in the black and silver top, with the hips—my goodness, lovely.*

A rush of sweat pooled on the sides of his nose. He wiped at it between strums, and nearly dropped the pick from his slick fingers. The four standing around the table over to the right weren't paying attention—he'd stare at them and see if they'd notice. One of them did and shushed the others. Rudy allowed himself a slight smug flush of victory.

They say find what you love and let it kill you:
No, find what you love and let it keep you alive
The dawn leapt from its bed and dissolved the stars
We went from counting our blessings to counting cars
And the bars on the window
Anything to keep our heads from our pillows
I wanted to write you a glad song, but I didn't have time
So I wrote you a sad one
And made gods of garlic and vine

There was a cloudburst of applause and a few lightning-strike whistles. A young man in a flat cap yelled, "That was a good song!"

Rudy showed his teeth and squinted into the house lights. "That was a great heckle."

PABLO STOOD BY the monitor desk as Rudy, ruddy with triumph, stumbled past, a hasty snarl of cables wedged under his arm.

"Hey!" Pablo aimed a wrist at Rudy. "It's 9:18. You're off at 9:15."

"Oh," Rudy faltered. "Sorry man, I lost track. Thought I could squeeze seven tunes in. Not bad, though, huh?"

"We're on a schedule. Wear a watch." He turned away and briefly conferred with dreadlocked Jackie, on her way to replace the house mic with Ryan's personal one. Dismissed, his pride punctured, Rudy continued to the dressing room.

Ryan was standing, facing a corner, whispering something to himself. Rudy turned to give him his preparatory privacy, but his hip knocked the mini-fridge, and three half-empty beer bottles fell like bowling pins and rattled off the wall and onto the floor. Ryan spun around, then relaxed a little. "Rudy!" he said brusquely. "Great set—"

"Thanks—"

"—ran a little over, though. Anyway, you'll get the hang of it." Ryan turned to a mirror and ran his hands through his hair, turned his head left and right and looked back at Rudy. "Why don't you come sing on something tonight?"

"I don't know," said Rudy. "I felt pretty good out there. Don't want to confuse the issue."

"Well, think on it for tomorrow," said Ryan. "I want these kids to get a good look at you. Tee you up for success, you know?" He flattened the front of his shirt with his hands. "OK, I gotta go do this." He jumped up and down, twice, exhaled loudly, and strode toward the stage.

The house lights crashed out, some pomposity with organ and choir crested on, and the impersonal baying undertow in the room greeted Ryan's silhouette. He raised a beer bottle in modest contrast and began, a relaxed conductor following a familiar score: "Hi, everybody. This one's called 'Don't Let's Go Crazy (No, Let's Go Crazy).'" He set the bottle at his feet. *"Want so much more than I got!"*—a downbeat strum, cheers of recognition—*"I got so much that I don't want!"*—hundreds of voices in unison halo around his, a field of raised fists like sunflowers in the light.

12

RUDY AWOKE IN his bunk. Or was he fully awake? He probed the edges of his compromised consciousness. He skimmed over trigger points of shame and envy. The benefit of tying one on the first night of tour, his reasoning went, is that you get a tactile reminder of your limitations, and then you can calibrate. By night three or four he'd achieved a nice equilibrium: neither peak performance nor shamefully debilitated, just that midtour functional crappiness. In any case, it was difficult to speak in terms of "a good night's sleep" in the submarine coffin of the bunk. Nights of accumulated cold sweat effused from the pillowcase. Every time he rolled over, he kneed the carpeted roof and got an angry grunt from Jackie, entombed above. A vent by his feet blew icily at unpredictable intervals, punctuating the choking airlessness and stagnant farts.

The bunks were stacked in three rows—floor-level, middle, and upper—two sets of three to the left and two to the right for a total of twelve, with sluggish pocket doors at each end which kept the windowless corridor in a permanent state of twilight. Ring-hung sliding curtains protected each person's privacy, which was strictly respected to shelter the solitary needs of involuntary celibates.

The floor-level bunk seemed like a choice spot—rolling in and out would be quick and easy, and, since there were no ladders, he would keep his feet out of other people's beds and theirs out of his. Whether it was better to be closer to the front or back lounge, there was no smart play: the drinkers sat up in the front by the fridge, the weed smokers in the back with the video games, and either were just as likely to be loud or up late. The rumble and ambient noise of moving wheels was the only sure sedative, the herky-jerky rite of early morning parking the signal that any further sleep would be provisional. The permanent darkness in the bunk meant he couldn't know whether it was three a.m. and he should roll over (sparing Jackie's kidneys) and go back to sleep, or whether it was noon and he'd missed load-in.

Rudy's phone rested in a net pocket on the carpeted wall. He stuck a finger through the interwoven cords and pressed a button on its side. The screen lit up. A small envelope nested beneath the readout of the time: 9:38, neither dully early nor embarrassingly late. He pulled the phone up over the elastic lip and flipped it open.

Rudy! it's Selima from savannah. i wanna come see you an ryan 2nite in stl can you put me on the list plus one?let's hang out too long time

He'd stayed with that couple with the arbor, Rudy recalled. They sat in a circle and smoked. The husband excused himself early, and the wife edged closer. A good friend of theirs had just died of cancer, she said, opening a wooden drawer. Before the undertakers and the ambulance arrived, they'd secured the terminal pain medication. They spread out the take: small bottles and Fentanyl patches. Selima, the couple's friend from Savannah—

plump, bowtie mouth, faded green dots dancing on the flesh around her thumb—placed her hand surreptitiously over Rudy's. Later, after her boyfriend had gone to bed, she kissed him chastely on the balcony.

He'd seen Selima a couple more times over the years in whatever town she happened to be in. Sometimes they'd taken off more clothes, sometimes not, sometimes they'd done more and different drugs, sometimes not. He'd thickened, so had she. One of those see-you-next-year relationships. At this point, it seemed like they wouldn't sleep together, but then why did they keep getting these dinners when he came through? He wasn't even sure he wanted to, anymore, beyond the obscure balm of checking off unfinished business.

> Oh hey yeah i'll have sound check so cant get dinner but text me when you get to the venue

Tap-tap tap-tap tap-tap-tap for yes, tap-tap pause tap-tap-tap for no: the Morse-code reflex of spelling messages into flip phones. Rudy rolled through the curtain onto the nappy hallway floor, grunted to his feet, and slid the hatch open. The last tar of a pot of coffee sizzled and puffed. Rudy tested the carafe with the back of his hand. Satisfied, he filled a mug that read "I Survived the Great Blow Explosion of 2000": crew jokes. With a paper towel, he swept the dry mouse-droppings of spilled grounds from the counter into his damp hand. A muffled, tinkling inanity chimed from the pocket of his pants. He pulled out the phone again, flipped it open with one hand, and grabbed the coffee with the other. He yanked the antenna with his teeth and exited through the exhaling front door, squinted away the sun.

"Lauren."

"Hey Rude. How's rock-and-roll finishing school with your star pupil?"

Rudy gulped from the mug and spit stray bitter grounds from his tongue. "The pupil doesn't need my advice anymore, it looks like. Maybe I've got something for these kids that come see him, though."

"OK, Father Time. You're twenty-nine."

"Fine, but a generation in rock is five years. Like, the difference between in high school and in college, between in college and in bars. That's when people hit reset on their taste. So Ry's got all these fifteen-, sixteen-year-olds in tight pants and shiny hair and awkward love. He's like their older brother who can talk them through their problems. He'll sit at the edge of the stage after the house lights are up and listen to them, sign shit, hugs, pictures. He'll come back to the bus with a handful of their zines and poems and hand-decorated CD-Rs. He radiates such a fundamental decency it's kind of exhausting to be around."

"And—I say this as your sister—you radiate a kind of low-level hostility."

"I just . . . I don't know. No one's ever reacted to my songs like that."

"Except him."

"Yeah. Except him."

They sat for a while in the silence.

"Rudy," she said finally. "I didn't just call to rub tiger balm on your ego. Jules and I are—I'm pregnant. Jules's gonna move up here."

Rudy stared across the parking lot. The bus was stationed beside a two-story dive faced with corrugated siding. Neon over the door boasted "24/7." It was the lone building in the middle of several acres of stained and sandy tarmac. Around the distant edges ran a railroad track; overlooking it a watchtower on stilts; past that the black exhaust towers of a chemical plant, behind the loom and lattice of an electrical switching station. "Jules is moving to Boston?"

"Yes, thank you, I accept your congratulations, we're very happy."

"Yeah, I mean, congratulations, but. What about your diss—?"

"—ertation? I talked to my advisor about it. She said that in a way it's better to have a baby while you're still in grad school. OK, you don't have much money, but your schedule is pretty flexible, and I'm just home writing most of the time right now anyway. Better to have a toddler who can be in nursery school if we're moving all the time for whatever post-docs or temporary appointments I can get after I graduate. And man, a newborn on top of the first couple years of a tenure-track, I dunno. I'll be pushing forty by the time I'm settled anywhere. This way seems better."

"OK," he said, with as little skepticism as possible. "I trust you. What's Jules going to do?"

"Change diapers and make me dinner, for now."

"Nice for him."

"Yes," Lauren said, "I'll have it harder. There's no way around that. Breadwinner and breastfeeder. That's what I won. But it's worth it to me to not have to do this alone. I like his company, and he does the dishes, and I won't have to put kids to bed every night. That's love."

"Is he there? Can I talk to him?"

"Sure, hang on." There was a rustling on the line, followed by a burst of static.

"Hey Rudy. How about that, huh?" Jules sounded—excited?

"It's something, man. Does Seb know?"

"We had a drink and a long talk last night. I mean, let's be real, is the band ever going to get any bigger than it is now? We've been playing the same places for the same people for a couple years now. Local heroes. There was a moment—but we never got to a place where anyone was making a living on it, and the moment passed. Now you're out half the time on your own, Cass has the restaurant and the politics, Seb—"

"Yeah, what about Seb?"

"You know Seb. You're either sworn to his program and he'd gut his mother for you, or you're in the ninth circle frozen in a block of ice. Anyway, I talked him down. Détente, right? I Jimmy Cartered that shit. But that guy will strap on a grudge and nuzzle it like a feedbag."

"He's still pissed at me about this tour?"

"What'd I just say? His ship's sailing shorthanded. To be honest, man, it's kind of a weight off. I see some of these guys who never quite break through and they're still on the road when they're forty-five, fifty, older, day-to-day style, it's a rough look. I mean, don't get me wrong, I can see you doing that. Liking it."

"Keep on doing it even if no one cares? Why would I—what good is singing songs if no one's listening?"

"My point is I think I'm grateful for the off-ramp. I mean, it doesn't mean I have to stop playing, right, there's bands in Boston."

"Are there?"

"Speaking of off-ramps, how's the bus?"

"Same bait, bigger boat. More time on my hands, since I'm not driving all day. We'll still get to the point where we only communicate with catchphrases and inside jokes."

Jules laughed. "And sobbing."

Once you pop the bubble, Rudy thought, you can't ever remember what was so comforting about its walls. "What are you going to do in Boston?"

"What Lauren said. She's got the, let's say, higher ceiling on her earning potential, so I'm just gonna try and make things easy for her for now. I'm calling midwives and shit. Reading up. Did you know they say you should eat the placenta? Like grind it up and put it in a smoothie, or fry it with some eggs."

"I thought you were vegan."

"I am, but how great to say, yeah, I don't eat meat, but I make an exception for *human flesh*!"

RUDY PUNCHED IN the code and reentered the bus. The front lounge had populated. Pablo was scowling through reading glasses at a sheaf of stapled papers. Jackie was microwaving her last night's half-eaten burger. She gave Rudy a nod.

"Morning, Jackie," said Rudy. "How'd you sleep?"

"Fine," she said in a nasal oboe tone, "once these animals finally settled down." She raised a hooped eyebrow at Cy and Max, who were slouched on opposite ends of a bench seat in matching black-on-black mufti, with carabiners jingling keys from their belts. Cy, his folds of fat stretching his too-tight shirt, was intent on a video game; Max, slim and reading a glossy guitar magazine. They had been Ryan's childhood buddies. Max was in Ryan's band, when he toured with one. Cy, Ryan said, was just fun to have around—the social lubricant. A vibesman.

"Take it ease," Max retorted. "Late load-in today. Roadie Friday."

"We got here at four in the morning," said Jackie to Rudy, "and I don't know if you've checked this place out yet, but it never closes. That's why the concrete blast barriers all around the building, so drunks don't drive through the wall. These two went right to work."

"Yeah, picturesque location," said Rudy. "Nature's wonders."

"Freaking surface of the moon."

"C'mon, Cy," said Max, tossing his magazine on the table. "Let's go on walkabout. Explore this craphole."

"They got Waffle House in this shit?" Cy asked, without taking his eyes off the screen.

"I think Waffle House is only in the South," said Max.

"St. Louis ain't the South?"

"Remind me how the Missouri Compromise turned out again?"

"They musta covered that after I dropped out. But if they got a Waffle House it's the South, I don't care what side they were on. Let's go stimulate the local economy. Help 'em rise again." Cy stuck the controller sideways in a cutout drink holder and groaned up from the couch. "Jackie, ya wanna go for a roam?"

"Nah, I gotta repollute my system with this atrocity," she said, as the microwave chimed. "Godspeed."

Cy gave her a mock-courtly bow, and they flapped through the curtain. Rudy dipped into the booth seat and picked up Max's discarded magazine.

"Pablo," Jackie said, with a mouthful of steaming burger, "you get down with the Waffle House?"

Pablo crossed a line off a list of figures. He put down his pen and looked up. "My dad left my mom for a Waffle House waitress."

"Sounds like a country song," said Jackie sympathetically.

"So I guess Waffle House is kind of ruined for you," said Rudy.

Pablo gave it a beat. "I *love* Waffle House."

From behind the door to the bunks came a click, then a peremptory yank, followed by the dull thud of a knee and a muffled curse. Jackie reached over and turned the handle. Ryan yawned his way into the light. "Jesus fucking I can never get that door right. Morning everybody."

Yup, mm-hmm, er.

"Hey Rudy," Ryan said, shaking the empty coffee pot with disappointment. "Rose called. She emailed you some album press she wants you to read."

"Don't have a computer."

"You can borrow mine, it's in my bunk. I bet you can get online in the venue office."

Ryan's laptop in hand, Rudy entered the empty club. The bartender left off slicing limes and led him to an attic warren under bare rafters. Against its back wall groaned chrome shelving nearly lost beneath a pile of padded tan packing envelopes: booking requests from bands, hundreds of them. So this is where those dreams go to gather dust, Rudy thought. There was just enough room to swivel the duct-taped chair around to face a candy-colored computer, which sat on a sheet of plywood supported by a pair of filing cabinets. He pushed aside some grimy comic-book figurines and four disconnected pads of Post-It notes, and pawed at the back of the monitor for the ethernet cable. He snapped it into the scuffed white plastic molding of Ryan's laptop, logged onto his email, and opened the message from Rose. *Rudy— here's the* Haystack *review.* He clicked the link, and a browser window unfurled.

RUDY PAUVER
The Morris Column
(Bad Dream)
6.8
Arguably best known as the former bassist for semilegendary Gainesville strivers the Expats, Rudy Pauver has reinvented himself as the best of Bad Dream Records' new stable of Ryan Orland protégées. The Florida-by-way-of-the-upper-Midwest troubadour's sophomore

solo outing is a set of overdetermined, oblique poems with a sense of autumn turning, a far cry from his mentor's seminal emo heroics despite their sonic similarities.

Where Orland's rollicking, passionate songs rage and cajole, Pauver's overwritten and performatively allusive lyrical content (which easily overshadows his workmanlike fingerpicking) sidesteps into blank verse. In fact, in opener "When Language Goes Walking," he explicitly compares the "walking language" of prose to "dancing language" of poetry (and by extension, presumably, song). "Gates of Fame, Gates of Envy" and the title track seem to obscurely outline his relationship with his mentor, and dense tracks like "A Chemistry of Stars," "Bee of the Moment," and "Bring Fever, Bring Farm" are frankly undecipherable. "My Straight-To-Cable Dreams" and "Your Jesuitical Lover" are welcome returns to more recognizable narrative, while "Garlic and Vine" is a lovely valentine.

The coffeeshop-balladeer-meets-the-OED pretension of the project quickly tires, though, and it's hard to imagine who the audience is: the Venn diagram of comp-lit grad students and diehard Orland bootleggers presumably exists, but whether it's enough to sustain the newcomer is an open question. Pauver needs to absorb some of Orland's common touch as well as his voice if he's going to take his own seat at the table.

Rudy felt a hot wave rush from his face to tingle the tips of his fingers. He clicked back to the email from Rose: *Could be better,* she said, *but we'll get 'em next time. Working on more.* He smacked the laptop closed and yanked the cable from the side. He pummeled down the curling staircase and hip-checked through the door into the sunlight. He called Cass and began to rant, pacing the lot-side crabgrass. Fucking name-droppers, bootlickers, bandwagon manufacturers and bandwagon arsonists, time's flies, minute-jacks, hucksters of prefab language, with their subliterate so-called editors, whiplashing between flattering-courtier overstatement and mock-pitying, multihyphenate condescension—

"Am I wrong," she tried to interrupt, "or is it not entirely a bad review?"

"—as if they've ever done anything, what a joke, parasites and mediocrities, they always will be, too concerned with curating and exhibiting their own taste to ever risk anything. How dare they give me advice, as if they have any idea—"

"Rudy, I'm sorry," she said. "They may be wrong about your relationship with Ryan, but—"

"—yes they fucking *are* wrong, and like is this how it's going to *be* now, like I'm the *apprentice* who needs *tutoring,* like he wasn't a *teenager* and there's not even a fucking like *complaints* department with these people—"

"—but they're not wrong about the difference between you guys. His songs are tools for the people who need them. Yours want people to come and decode them. Like, when he says he's hurting, he just says it, you know? Songs are for people to use. Plus, Rude, I love you, but come on, he looks like a sad earnest little chipmunk angel, and you look like a potato that's taken some punches."

"They don't even know what 'blank verse' is. Fuckin' cretins."

"You're a snob."

"I'm an elitist, it's different. I demand a jury of my peers."

"OK, I retract. You're a secret egotist."

"Secret! I get on stage for a living."

"A living!"

"A vocation."

"An avocation. What I do at the restaurant is a living."

"You play drums."

"Not anymore, remember? Lauren called me, too."

"It doesn't have to be—"

"But it is. Everyone knows it. Even Seb, that's what he's so mad about. Anyway, Rudy, I wanted to talk to you about something else. I'm going to Iowa next week. I'll be there—well, through January at least."

"For Dean? This is your new savior? Fucking hell. Didn't you learn any lesson four years ago when your guy elected this happy moron?"

"Fuck you, first; second, that's not what happened; third, ideals are not subject to lessons, as you put it, talk about condescending."

"But I'll be home in three weeks."

"Yes, you will. I won't be."

13

RUDY TOOK THE stage that night, and the crowd wobbled and tittered like a dropped coin. It was clear, looking out, that they found him a little too old, a little too dull, a little too quiet, a little too ignorant of, or indifferent to, their needs. Clear that they liked that he sounded like what they liked; but it wasn't enough, his gentle fingerpicking, the dynamic sameness of his songs, the obscurity of the lyrics. That maybe sometimes when he strummed they could hear a rowdy song straining to emerge from the timid tunes, but that his affect was too muted to make an impression from a big stage, without an audience preraptured. *My project fails, which was to please.* He tried commanding, but the bored and distracted crowd had a cumulative power no amplification could overcome. He tried the softly, softly: he backed off the mic and stroked the strings. A few people in the front ten feet turned and shushed behind them, and there was a brief lull of shame and annoyance, but those who turned their attention back to Rudy clearly found themselves no more captivated than before, and resumed their conversation. Rudy saw Ryan, in the wings, whisper something to Pablo, turn and disappear up the green-room stairs.

Rudy swallowed waves of hurtling anger. In their troughs came mortification, and finally disgust. He skipped last verses, spit through end rhymes, and elided climaxes. He paused to introduce a next song, then just grunted, looked down, began. He sang quieter and retreated further, and finally, simply, quit. He yanked the cable from the heel of his guitar, dragged the unlatched case flapping behind him, and left the stage to scant scattered mosquito-sting claps from those who noticed.

As he passed Jackie, Pablo stepped in front of him. Rudy looked past his shoulder but Pablo put out a hand. Rudy stopped and looked at him, annoyed that his self-pity was being derailed.

"It's 9:05," said implacable Pablo. "You've got ten minutes left. We're a week in, how come you can't get your fucking set times right?"

"It's over. It doesn't matter. They don't give a shit."

"Maybe not, but I do. We're on a schedule here. I got house music timed out so they can get a drink and be restoked for Ryan after your glum ass. I thought you were supposed to be an old pro. Write a fucking set list. Al can get out thirty minutes on the nose, so can you."

"Al plays the same set every night."

"Buddy," said Pablo, "maybe you don't know this, but management didn't want you on this tour. I don't know who the fuck you are. Doesn't look like you're bringing much to the table, draw-wise. Ryan insisted on you. So why don't you ask yourself whether you think this is an opportunity, a victory lap, or a last chance. And make sure you're being honest."

As Jackie and Max weaved around them to reset the stage, Rudy took advantage of their blocking to edge away. Pablo turned his attention to the backdrop—a woodcut hunting horn, hanging from the letterpress "y" in "Ryan Orland"—swaying in front of the upstage drape.

The crowd's attention sucked into Ryan and his wild trumpet voice and his bulging temples and his romances. Rudy could hear a scrap of his patter, distorted and distant with echo: "I want to thank my old buddy Rudy Pauver for coming out with us. Rudy and I have known each other for a long time. He's been a huge part of making me who I am, and we're thrilled to have him in the Bad Dream family. Let's give him a round of applause." The ambient buzz surged a little and subsided. "And how about that Al Pashlo!" The swell rose a little higher, and Rudy escaped to the vast dark parking lot. The flare stacks illuminated the brutal parapet of the horizon.

Rudy didn't smoke. Never saw the point. The cost-benefit ratio was all wrong. Something that bad for you, he figured, had better get you really fucking high, and not, like, the equivalent of a good cup of coffee. But sometimes it was a little hard to know what else to do in a scene like this, which seemed to demand leaning against the outer wall of the club and lighting a cigarette.

A lean man with sallow custard skin and a white ponytail leaned against the outer wall of the club next to Rudy and lit a cigarette. He offered the pack. "No thanks," said Rudy. "Anything that bad for me had better get me way fucking higher." After all, that was his line.

The man put the cigarettes back in the breast pocket of his flannel shirt. "I was gonna ease into it," he said. "But since you mention it, I got those, too."

Rudy looked at him, his worn carpenter boots, the frayed fringe of his jeans, the red plaid hanging loose over a white tank top. "Like what specifically?"

"I got the stuff that keeps you from hanging out here by yourself like you're posing for a painting, instead of inside having a good time with what look to me like some cute and may I say appreciative girls."

A muted cheer seeped out the propped-open door. Rudy's phone jangled some coins in his pocket. He pulled it out, held it down by his hip, and snapped it open with a thumb. Selima: *hey sorry jes got here did we miss your set?*

"You want my advice," said the guy, "don't take 'em like pills. Take a liter of water, like that electrolyte water maybe, why not get out in front of the recovery, add a packet of vitamin C powder 'cause ditto, and dissolve the pills in that. Then you can just sip on it. You don't get that blow-your-hair-back crest, but like a steady mellow maintenance glow. I'm Beau, by the way."

"Man, I tried to regulate like that on a tour once," said Rudy, shoving the phone back in his pocket. "I set up a little minibar next to me on stage, on my amp, with a cup of coffee, a Jameson, couple beers, a Red Bull, some waters, so I could, like, take stock after each song and micromanage my buzz." Rudy held out his right hand sideways. "Nice to meet you, Beau."

Beau grunted, shifted his cigarette from his right hand to his lips, and shook. "Mm-hmm. How'd that work for you?" he muddled through the available side of his mouth.

"Fucking terrible. Hammered every night."

Beau sniffed his concurrence. "But that's like chemical interactions between different substances—this is just re-upping the one. I've been doing it with mushrooms myself, making a like tincture, like a dropperful. I was really fuckin' down, you know, for a long time, and it just helped with the lethargy and I just feel more centered, and like clarity."

"Clarity."

"Yeah, but the only thing is it'll just give you a little . . . *leeeaaan* when you're trying to stand still."

Rudy felt like he was having a little trouble standing up as it was. "Alright, fuck it," he said. "Hook me up."

"Great," said Beau. "Follow me."

He moved with a focused lope, calculatedly casual but dead serious. Rudy followed a pace behind. Their destination, he realized, was a silver pickup parked alone in a far corner of the lot.

"Little exposed, isn't it?" said Rudy.

"Nah. Nobody around here. Hop in"—Beau turned the key and the black golf-tee locks popped up—"it's open."

Rudy hoisted himself up, one hand on the vinyl seat, one on the door handle, and slid in. The seats had raw haybale scars and the cab smelled of must and spilled soda. "Yeah," he said, gesturing at the gas flares from the factory. "What the hell happened around here, anyway?"

"Bull rats and brownfields, my man. The Bluffs and the Bottoms. Race riots over jobs that were gonna leave anyway. Fuckups in shitty hall. They call this St. Louis, but the real St. Louis is on the other side of the river, and Springfield doesn't give a shit."

"You live here?" Rudy asked.

"Fuck no. Those smokestacks alone will kill ya. They got no hospital, no supermarket, fuckin' the streetlights aren't even on. They got like homemade stop signs tied onto the poles. That strip club over there is probably the biggest business in town. Fuckin' tear it all down and start over." Beau reached beneath the seat and scrabbled around for a few seconds. "ATMs that give tens, though. Anyway, here's what I got for you."

He pulled out a half-gallon screw-top Mason jar, comically larger than the two Ziploc bags neatly folded at its bottom. "Shrooms forty for an eighth, E's ten per. Fuck it, dozen for a hundred."

"Can't resist a deal," said Rudy. He counted off five twenties. Almost half his pay for that night, but then again, he hadn't played much more than half a set.

"Good man. You got it." Beau reached behind the seat this time and found a smaller jar. He decanted twelve white pills— plink, plonk, ting, tang—screwed the lid tight and handed it rattling to Rudy. Rudy looked eye-level through it at the club's neon, distorted and flared in the glass.

Beau flipped down the driver's-side sun visor and pulled a torn envelope from the elastic. He looked at both sides. He took a pen, branded "Corporate America Family Credit Union," from the ashtray, wrote a number on the flap, tore it off, unscrewed the lid of the Mason jar, and dropped the scrap in with the pills. "Customer satisfaction is important to me. You let me know how these treat you. Ever come back through St. Loo, you call me up."

They shook hands and Rudy let himself out. He looked at the glass jar in his hand. He tried to shove it in the pocket of his jeans, then tried curling it hidden in his palm. He forced it down the inside breast pocket of his jacket, looked down at the tumorous lump, shook his head, and walked past the lone security guard with his coat held, he hoped, inconspicuously and casually wide.

Backstage, he unscrewed the lid, shook two pills into his hand, clapped his hand to his open mouth, and flushed them down with the dregs of a nearby beer. He picked up a matchbox, slid out the drawer, dropped six more pills next to the leftover strike-any-wheres, and put it all back in his pocket. Then he closed the jar, stuffed it in his suitcase, and covered it with some underwear. He entered the number in his phone under the name "Beau Pills." He crumbled the scrap of envelope and threw it behind a broken-backed couch.

SELIMA, AND A FRIEND, were waiting in the front of the bar, near the folding table that held the merch. On it, binderclipped to white portable racks strung with Christmas lights, were Ryan's five T-shirt designs, three records in an assortment of formats and designs, various seven-inches, stickers, special editions, bandanas, beer coozies, and branded errata. They crowded Al Pashlo's ambitious offerings and elbowed aside Rudy's limited ones: a CD-R of *Flamed Amazement*, a CD and LP of *The Morris Column*, and a sheet of printer paper Sharpied "Rudy Pauver Mailing List" across the top. The pen had already been stolen.

Rudy felt an acceleration, his senses starting to hiss and crackle around the edges.

Rudy! she said—fingerless leather motorcycle gloves, black hoodie under matching jean vest trimmed with chrome studs and garnished with white-on-black fabric patches. What's up man, so sorry we missed your set, you know how it is, oh this is Miss Elin, yeah, Selima and Elin, like two crazy old bats ha ha.

"Hey Elin," he said, "I'm Rudy, nice to meet you. Here, I got a couple of drink tickets, what do you two want?" He waved down a bartender and ordered three gin and tonics. He turned back to Selima. "So, what are you doing in St. Louis?"

"I got a dog-sitting gig and just stayed for now. More tornados but way less floods—cheers—so."

"So."

"So, good to see you, how's the tour going?"

"Fine, I guess, you know, they're his crowds, but they're OK, not my first rodeo, I can give a Roland for an Oliver or an Oliver for Orlando or whatever the phrase is."

"A Rudy awakening."

"Ha ha, good one. So Elin, how long you been here?"

Her voice was like a wheezy pump organ unused to being played. "Oh, I ended up here after I left Idaho, like when my bus money ran out and just stayed."

Rudy nodded too fast, bobbing, his brain thrusting against the confines of his skull, the room, space and time. "Hey, listen they're wrapping up it sounds like, what are you guys up to later?"

"We're at the ABV across the river," said Selima. "You want to come over and have some drinks?"

"Not too far, I hope."

"Like ten minutes over the bridge, not even, we'll take my car."

"Yeah, why not, and by the way, I got some other stuff if you want, I don't know if you want, but—" He pulled out the matchbox.

"Fuck yeah, man, make a night of it." Selima laughed. "Want to see if Ryan wants to come too?"

"Maybe," said Rudy, "I mean he does all that pictures and signing business, so it'll be an hour or so but I'll see. Why don't you guys hang here for a few minutes?"

Cy and Max had packed up the stage and gotten into the backstage beers and cold nachos, tag teaming their way down the scripts of familiar road gags.

"—and the Hoover Dam, right, like a tent city security station, they had like a generator and a fridge and a fan and a can of Raid—"

"—and there was a thermometer like strapped to the poles holding the tent up, right? Like a hundred twenty degrees—"

"—yeah, and the cop opened the side door of the van and wanted to open up the road cases, and Ryan was like, aw, man, that's kind of hard to get to, we pack from the back—"

"—yeah, and the cop was like, sir, we're the Department of Homeland Security, we're the last line of defense for the dam—"

"—ha ha and you said, sir, the only thing I terrorize is pussy!"

Laughter. "Ah shit. Good times."

Ryan emerged from a shower closet, barefoot in jeans and towel-scrubbed hair. He pulled the same sweaty T-shirt from his show back over his head. "Rudy, you're back, I thought we lost you tonight, light out for the territories and all that. Rough one huh?"

"Oh that," said Rudy, giddy, "man, yeah, but you know fuck them, fuck them, pearls for pigs."

Ryan looked at him funny. "Hey, you know, those are my people out there."

But Rudy skated past the look, giggled: "The people of the island, huh, sounds and sweet airs that give delight and hurt not—"

"What?" said Ryan.

"Oh, nothing," said Rudy.

"You're in good spirits."

"I got some friends in town," said Rudy, "this girl I know from Savannah and her friend. You want to come out with us?"

"Around here?" said Ryan. "Where the fuck would we go? I'm not, like, a strip club kind of guy."

"Nah, just a hotel room jam."

Ryan looked at Pablo, Pablo shrugged his indifferent permission.

"Fuck it, sure," said Ryan.

And then they were all four packed in Selima's car, the girls in front ka-chunking the tape deck and Ryan and Rudy in the back seat covered with dog hair.

"Sorry about all the garbage," said Selima over her shoulder. "Just push it on the floor."

"Hey Ry," said Rudy, "you want one of these?"

"Oh, is that why everyone's so peppy. Ha ha, jeez, thanks but no thanks, it's only week one, marathon not a sprint right?"

"Shit man, what's the point of being a big rock dude?"

"It's a job, Rude, like, a lot of people are counting on me."

"Oh like a CEO; clean living, that's what this is all about, huh?"

And then they were through a lemon-scented lobby up a mirrors-in-mirrors elevator and bouncing off the walls of the sound-sucking hallway, *who's got the key, I got the key, shit the key doesn't work here, let me, ha ha I can never do those stupid things—*

"—who wants a drink, we just have this." Selima held up a plastic handle of gin and some coffee mugs. "No mixers, sorry."

"I can get some sodas from the machine," said Ryan.

"Ah, we don't need it," said Rudy.

"OK," said Selima. "Four warm gins coming right up." She turned to Ryan. "You know, I'm allergic to vodka."

"I never heard of that," Ryan said.

"Yeah, I break out in a good time!" She cackled.

Rudy thought Selima looked pretty good after all, the little leather belt-purse sitting back on her hip, though how was this all going to work, the four of them in this hotel room, anyway he'd done sketchier shit, like remember sharing a room with Jules who was on the floor with that med student whispering about I think you'd be more comfortable with your pants off, or the rhythmic rustle of the shower curtain from behind the closed door while everyone pretended to sleep, or like roaming hands in the van while the rest slept inside then shivering on the bench seats all night; actually that time was sort of sweet, we squatted on the sidewalk and held hands while everyone filed out in the morning, anyway just see what happens—*yeah, pour me another one, thanks*—be funny to see what Ryan's up for, where's his bad self live, y'know, where's the evil in him, mister I'm-just-like-them, mister I'm-an-overgrown-good-kid, you spend too much time playing shows for teenagers you forget you're not one of them, you cling to their pitiless values, they're not your peers; I know what my sin is, it's judgment, and envy I guess, you have to know your specific shittiness so it doesn't surprise you, you need your saturnalia, everybody's got their mutually agreed upon vice, right, Americans with their guns and gluttony, Germans got speeding and self-righteousnessness; come on, Ry-guy, show me you're a real boy after all, let yourself do something cruddy and weird.

But Selima was sitting on the arm of Ryan's chair now, telling him in her funny fluty voice about how she was part Native American, about her plans for the eclipse coming up, that she and Elin were going to hike to the top of the hill by their house and paint their faces and strip naked and do some kind of improvised spiritual cleansing thing.

"Uh-huh," said Ryan.

"Yeah," said Elin, and everyone looked at her.

"Elin just got a new job," said Selima.

"Oh yeah," said Ryan.

"Yeah," said Elin, "I was doing, like, well they call it an erotic chat line, from home for a while. But I just got a job at an insurance call center."

"She can use the same skills," said gleeful Selima. "For information about mammograms press one, squeeze them giant titties, ha ha!"

Elin looked a little embarrassed.

"Well, she's a recovering Mormon," said Selima. "We're still working on her."

"No shit," said Rudy.

"Yeah," said Elin, "up in Idaho, like everyone in my family thought the apocalypse was coming when it looked like Gore would win, my parents were crying when Fox called Oregon, my brother sent a mass email saying he could get us cheap guns if we needed, I said he probably shouldn't say that since he works for Boise police but you know."

"Shit," said Ryan.

"Yeah," said Selima, "like her parents have enough food in their house for thirty people for a month."

"All their friends know they can come there," said Elin.

"She still carries a seventy-two-hour bag," said Selima.

"What's that," said Rudy.

"All of us do," said Elin, "a go bag, a backpack in my bedroom that has canned food, changes of clothes, a straw that filters water. My grandma has four guns in her car, one in the glovebox, one under each seat, one in the trunk. I found one reaching under the passenger seat for a pen, I said Grandma there's a gun here! She said I know, they may want to rape me!"

"Yeah but watch out for her," said Selima, "Elin, tell 'em about the animal sanctuary—no, she doesn't wanna, ha ha, she got fired from the animal sanctuary 'cause she trained a wolf to attack this coworker she hated." Selima leaned into Ryan's shoulder. "We both have atypical tongues, aaahhh, show 'em Elin, aaahhh, ha ha, did I get your ear Ry, oops, yeah geographic tongue they call it, like a map and little islands, oh you wanna visit, Orland on my islands, ha ha."

Ryan looked pleased and not surprised, and relaxed back into her.

"Selima, you need a refill?" Rudy said, rising and walking toward her, hand out for a cup.

"Nah, I'm good," she said, waving him off with the hand that wasn't now on Ryan's shoulder, Ryan who didn't look up, distracted briefly by his phone.

"I'll have a little," said Elin from the bed behind.

Rudy turned and looked at her: not the talkative one, tall with straight over-blond hair and some late acne on her face and her bare legs, sitting pretty straight and staring pretty straight too. Without looking at him she held out her mug, he took it and filled it gurgling from the jug and handed it back to her and turned back to the chair, where Ryan's hand was now on Selima's thigh. How lush and lusty he looks, with eye of green, thought Rudy, his head spiraling, ebullient, gleeful; there almost wasn't room for the angry gin but it kept elbowing its way up, poke poke jab, anyway his mouth wouldn't stay shut.

"Hey Ryan," he said, "I bet they've got an ice machine on this floor, c'mon, let's get a bucket so we can drink cold liquor like grown-ups."

"Nah," said Ryan, "you go get some man, I'm all settled in."

"I said c'mon, man, come with me, I gotta talk to you."

"Fuckin' Rudy, mister subtlety," said Selima, annoyed.

But Ryan said fine, Jesus; said to Selima I'll be right back, and got up and grabbed the ice bucket, exasperated, alright let's do this, and pushed past Rudy, clanked the door open, and stepped out into the chemical smell of the corridor.

The bare brightness slapped some of the edge off Rudy's plans, but still.

"So what's your problem," Ryan said.

"I know it's like tight quarters in there," said Rudy, "but maybe you want to take Elin on a walk or something."

"Elin," said Ryan.

"Yeah," said Rudy. "You know, me and Selima have a little history."

"Huh, does she know that," said Ryan.

"Look," said Rudy, "OK, the bathroom or the other bed, let's get weird."

"It's already weird," said Ryan. "What is this, Rudy, like a test or something?"

"C'mon Ryan, don't tell me you've been out all this time and never got into some scumbag shit."

"What are we, pirates like divvying up the booty?"

"Ha ha, yeah, right," said Rudy, pleased, understood.

"Jesus Christ, man, let's just get some ice and go back in there—"

"—what the *fuck* Ryan"—and the hug-it-out of the pills succumbed to the fight-it-out of the gin and Rudy shoved him with both hands up against the ice machine, which shivered, and a rattling avalanche collapsed inside it.

"Hey Rudy?" said Ryan. He grabbed Rudy's wrists and pulled them down and off his shirt. "I'm gonna go."

A SHORT MARCH, the scrunch of their soles on tight carpet, and they were back in the room. Selima was messing with a laptop, putting some music on. Elin now lay back with one knee up and her skirt a little open.

"You guys get it all sorted out," Selima said mockingly, "who gets who?"

"It's been really nice meeting you both," said Ryan, gave Selima a half-hug, cheeks together. "I come through a lot, next time, let's hang out, you let me know." He waved at Elin, she nodded, and he left without looking at Rudy.

"Well shit," said Selima. "Nice one Rudy, real cool."

But Rudy was still bubbling with adrenaline and serotonin and the idea that he had just won something—had he just won something?—and lay down on the floral bedspread gone slick with age. Elin turned her head, about level with his chest now, and looked up at him. He reached over to the nightstand for his mug of gin and slurped it sideways.

"Come on," he said to Selima, patting the empty side of the bed. "That guy's just green, doesn't know how to have a good time, let's just take it down a notch."

"Oh my God, are you for real," said Selima. "Like now we're gonna"—she looked at Elin, who was still looking at Rudy. "I see how it is. You guys do what you wanna, I guess. I'll just like be over here having a dignity party by myself." She turned up the music, beep *beep* BEEP went the volume too loud, and Elin sort of scooched up and raised herself on an elbow and looked at Rudy again and so he sat up and kissed her and they went from there. Elin still hadn't said much so he tugged on her skirt a little, it wouldn't move so she reached across her hip and opened a clasp and wriggled out of it herself and out of her underwear too, and Rudy sniffed a waft of the synthetic tang off the bedspread and stopped to sneeze.

"Bless you," said Elin.

Selima turned her back to them and leaned over the desk, cut off one song and started another, swung her hips a little and sang the opening lines. Florescent light and the congested racket of a fan blared from beyond the bathroom door. "You guys having *fun*," yelled Selima over the music, "does that feel *good*." Rudy sat up on his knees and unbuckled his belt, sat back and pulled off his jeans and shorts with one rattling motion, swept the small change that fell from his pocket onto the floor.

"You mind," he asked Elin apologetically. "I guess I'm a little fucked up, could you help me out," so she did. Selima went into the bathroom and ran the water in the sink. Elin lay back and pulled his forearm, pulled him up onto her. From the bathroom the scritch-scratch of a toothbrush and Selima's sarcastic commentary, foamy and muffled—"oh *yeah* y'all, fuckin' *go*"—spit—"for it." Elin's eyes were closed and her face was blank but her hands still pulled on his hips. Rudy looked up and beyond the bed and was distracted for a while by the dancing pink and purple swirls waving across the screen of Selima's computer. Selima stuck her head around the frame of the bathroom door, "hey big man, *focus*," so he did and it didn't take long after that.

"You guys ready to freak back in," said Selima, emerging from the bathroom in a worn T-shirt and plaid boxer shorts.

"Sorry," said Elin, who hadn't said anything in a while.

"You both wanted to get laid," said Selima, "far be it for me to *keep* you from it. Here." She tossed a rough white hand towel at Rudy, who wiped at his belly and the crook of his leg and handed it to Elin. Both still had their shirts on. Elin, towel in hand, looked questioningly at the tucked-tight bedspread.

"I mean, these things," said Rudy, "they only get washed once a week anyway."

"I think it's time for us to *turn in* if you don't mind," said Selima, "you know what I mean, Rudy," so he stood up, pulled his shorts and jeans back on with the one swift jerk, and hooked the buckle. He looked at cross-legged Elin and thought the thing to do was to give her a polite kiss but it didn't feel right and he saw she didn't think so either, so he gave her a kind of waist-level wave and said nice to meet you and she nodded and said nice to meet you too and he said see you next time Selima, fun party, and she said mm-hmm and looked at him until he was out the door and they were both still looking as the door clicked shut.

14

RUDY ROUSED LATE with a spike in his skull and acid in his gut and a buzzing numbness in his skin and a black shame, or a dull pride—his conscience hadn't figured out how to frame it yet. He rolled out of his bunk onto the hallway floor. The curtains of the other bunks were open and a few comforters hung limp. He stayed on his hands and knees for a long moment, looked up at the door and back down at the carpet. He took a deep breath and gathered himself upright, grabbing the middle bunks for support. He slid the door clunking to the side and winced as the sun amplified his headache.

"Mornin', sunshine," said Cy from the bench.

Rudy squinted out the side window. The bus was parked in an alley, with a couple feet to spare between the wall of a brick apartment tower on one side and the wall of a brick parking garage on the other. Two rusty dumpsters overflowed. The sky was blue and the clouds were white. Rudy lowered the corrugated curtain.

"Iowa City," said Pablo from his corner, without looking up.

"Ryan cabbed back early," said Cy. "The fuck did you get into? Happen with those girls?"

"Gentleman never tells," Rudy mumbled.

"Ah, sorry, buddy."

"Nah," said Rudy. "It got a little wild." He examined a selection of coffee mugs, determined that they were all used, and picked the cleanest-looking from the sink. His hands shook a little. His skin felt tender and raw.

"Multiples," said Cy approvingly. "Yeah man."

"Something like that." Until he figured out how he felt about the night, he'd let them think what they wanted.

"Sounded good last night," said Max. "You tapped out too soon. Fuck the haters."

Rudy relaxed, a little. Maybe the night—well, the show— hadn't been a train wreck.

"Ryan was looking for you," said Pablo. "He's in the back lounge."

"K," said Rudy. "Gimme a minute." The coffee, if it did anything, only cleared the haze that had protected him from a full accounting of himself—an accounting he now chose to postpone. He passed back through the dark hallway.

Ryan was seated in the back lounge, with an acoustic guitar on his lap, tucked under his armpits while he typed something into his computer. The windows were mercifully tinted. Mirrored, Ryan looked even more boyish than usual, and untouched by the night. Rudy's own reflection was less forgiving.

"Hey man," said Rudy. "Sorry about last night."

Ryan looked up at him, closed the laptop. He propped the guitar in the corner of the couch. "Yeah," he said. "Listen. I'm trying to run a professional operation here."

"I said, I'm sorry. Stuff makes me talk too much."

"Pablo says you're fucking up your set times every night. Says he keeps talking to you about it, but you don't give a shit."

Rudy paused, nonplussed. "Is *that* what this is about? Fuckin' seven songs or eight?"

"Everyone on this bus is trying to do their job and do it right, and you're disrespecting them and disrespecting me if you can't stay on point."

"I didn't realize you were the HR rep. C'mon, what is it, did that freak you out last night? It's sex. Farts and spasms. Sometimes it gets weird."

Ryan blinked at him. Rudy felt a distance; that Ryan was talking through him and past him. Rudy realized he had misunderstood something crucial about Ryan. Seeing Ryan as a blithe ingénue, he had wondered whether Ryan moved so fluidly in the world because it was so easy for him to fix things, or was it easy for him to glide past problems because he didn't dwell on them. Now he saw that an inflexible layer of detachment protected Ryan. Anything that threatened to become a problem for him took on an unreality that allowed it to glance off his bumper. And this bland management language was the arm's-length plow that cleared his path.

There was a subterranean rumble from the bays underfoot, like a calving iceberg, as the generator recycled. Ryan glanced at the walls just beyond the windows, first one side, then the other, then back at Rudy. "I was up early, Rudy. I've been trying to think how to say this. You know I've admired you for a long time. You were the one who was nice to me, let me hang around, taught me how to carry myself.

"I know you think I've taken something from you. I haven't. You just don't know how to take something from me. I understand. No one likes to be helped. You think it's too much like being in debt, debt that you can't ever get out from under, you can't just declare emotional bankruptcy. Or you think it's too much like pity, or guilt, something—it can't just be because I think you're talented and you meant something to me when I was a kid, and I thought then that if I ever had a chance, I wanted to give you a leg up, too."

Ryan was still sitting, and Rudy was still standing. Last night Rudy had surprised him, on neutral ground. Here was more clarity: he was an employee who had been called into Ryan's office.

"This, here"—Ryan gestured around him at the lounge, the bus, the club, his world—"this isn't a family, it's a team. I want you on my team. This is going to be quite a ride—Bad Dream, everything—it's gonna be big and it's gonna happen fast and I want you to be on it, too. But you have to be a team player."

"And every team has a captain," said Rudy.

"Yeah," said Ryan. He leaned forward, forearms on his knees. "It only works if everyone knows the rules and stays on the field. And I don't know if you're the kind of guy that stays on the field. Are you that kind of guy?"

Rudy felt the lounge contract around him. Ryan's eyes were now intent on his, focused and clear.

"No," Rudy said. "I guess I'm not."

Ryan sat back. "No. I didn't think so." He picked up a pair of outsized headphones and hung them around his bony shoulders. Their spiral cord ran across his heart and bounced gently. "Pablo already got you a plane ticket home. You're welcome to play tonight if you want to. But maybe you don't want to."

Ryan lifted the headphones' pads over his ears and turned his attention down to his computer. He smacked the space bar and began to sing quietly. No one likes to hear themselves sing. It never sounds like it does in their head, always a little thinner, a little weaker. Like it's someone else's voice entirely.

part IV

15

RUDY FLEW HOME, as Cass had promised, to an empty house. With Jules gone to Boston, Rudy drifted from room to room, unmoored from etiquette. He slept in his clothes on their bed. He slept naked on the couch. He spent a night on Jules's bare mattress, just to see how it felt. It smelled.

With nothing better to do, he got a job. The back seat of his car was soon redolent with flower deliveries, one through four for funeral homes, the next four to hospitals. The cycle of life running backwards, with gladioli at every downshift. The last bouquet went to a woman in her apartment, and they weren't from the guy who answered the door. Rudy quietly closed the door as the questions began.

He did, frankly, feel himself above delivery and restaurant work, and as soon as it felt physically and financially possible, he would go back on the road. There, at least, he wasn't in service of supercilious strangers and drunks ten years his junior, and could carry himself with a little dignity, even hauteur. Even on the worst nights, he was his own boss—if you didn't count the audience, which he didn't.

Cass called, occasionally, from Iowa. She was excited, distracted, committed; he was abstracted, indistinct, adrift.

REGNABO: The phone buzzed against their plywood bedframe.

"You're having a beer at 9:30 in the morning?" Cass asked from the kitchen door.

"Is that a weird thing to do?"

"It's an alcoholic thing to do."

Rudy hadn't considered it that way. "I just had a snack. I'm thirsty, and this is just what I like when I'm thirsty."

He rolled the top of the bag of tortilla chips, thought about clipping it, and shoved it upside down between two cereal boxes.

"Try seltzer next time. And chips aren't breakfast."

"I had breakfast at six when I got up."

"So have early lunch."

It was from Lauren, not Cass, that he expected this blunt candor, what she would have called an objective view of himself; and that in carefully limited doses, at a distance. But the little intimacies he treasured with Cass—reading to each other, locking eyes in the common embodiment of a rhythm section, the intellectual games that sparked their mutual attention and respect—were melting away. They stumbled on for almost another year, mostly because they were so rarely home at the same time. It wasn't that they didn't recognize what was happening, it was just that neither understood what the other was chasing.

"You change people by appealing to their hearts, not their minds," he said.

"Politics stiffens their resistance. Music breaks it down."

"I am appealing to their hearts," she said. "That's that thing you call idealism. If you nudge something forward politically, you change peoples' lives, materially; you don't just make them feel better, temporarily."

"Come with me and play drums. The Cass and Rudy show."

"You don't get it. You still care about something I no longer care about. I have no intention of becoming an art martyr. It's not noble, it's corroding you. Can't you tell? It's a horrible life; it makes it so you never have to grow up."

"It's a wonderful life; you never have to grow up."

REGNO: The phone buzzed against their plywood bedframe.

Rudy looked at the phone, didn't recognize the number, picked up anyway.

A bluff male voice: "Hi, can I speak to Rudy Pauver?"

"You can speak."

"Rudy, this is Frank Curton from Albatross Capital, how are you doing this morning?"

"My girlfriend is making grouchy noises, I knocked over my water glass, and I've got to piss like you wouldn't believe. How about you?"

"I'm sorry to hear that, Rudy. Now, Rudy, I'm calling because it says here you have a delinquent ChitCard balance in the amount of eight thousand, seven hundred and thirty-three dollars and nine cents, and I'm prepared to work with you on reasonable repayment terms. Now, Rudy, the—"

"I threw the card in the river."

"I'm sorry?"

"In the Monongahela River. In Pittsburgh. They have some lovely bridges there, and I took a long walk over one of them. About halfway across, I took my wallet out and I threw it over the guardrail. There wasn't anything in it I needed. It spread its wings and almost flew for a little while. All the cards sailed for a bit too. A mother bird and its cuckoo brood. Anyway, it didn't last. They float OK though. The Monongahela joins the Ohio, which flows to the Mississippi, jeez, it could be in Natchez by now. Better set up a dredge south of New Orleans."

"Mr. Pauver, the destruction of a physical card doesn't free you of the obligation to pay."

"If I break my hammer, you can't make me work."

"A credit card is not a tool, Mr. Pauver, and debt obligations aren't work."

"No? You sell it as a tool. Unlock the life you want and all that."

"I'm not with ChitCard, Mr. Pauver, I'm with Albatross Capital. We purchased your delinquent account."

"Fantastic. I don't owe anything to Albatross Capital."

"Can you confirm that you are refusing to pay?"

"I'm not refusing to pay. I would pay if I had the money."

"I understand things are difficult for you. How much do you think you can afford for a monthly payment?"

"Slice up my heart, measure out my blood."

"Sir?"

"I have a paper bag full of coins, mostly nickels, it looks like. And half a baguette. I still have to calculate taxes, but the rest can be yours."

"Mr. Pauver, I'm authorized to offer you a repayment amount of five thousand two hundred thirty-nine dollars and eighty-five cents, this is a forty percent reduction. If you can make a lump sum payment of five hundred dollars today I can lock in those terms—"

Rudy flicked the phone shut.

"Who was that?" Cass murmured.

"A maggot trying to feed on a mannequin," he said. He rolled toward the wall and started, quietly, to cry. She wrapped an arm around his chest from behind, and nuzzled herself into his back.

REGNAVI: The phone buzzed against their plywood bedframe.

"Ugh," said Cass as Rudy rolled over. "You got booze body. Aim that brewery elsewhere." She picked up his phone and looked at it.

Stella Dallas, it said. "*I need yooouuu*"

"Who the fuck is Stella Dallas?" said Cass.

"Someone named Stella I talked to after the Dallas show," Rudy said. "She said she wanted to make a poster for me, so I gave her my number."

That wasn't true. She'd grabbed Rudy's foot from the front row, and afterward brought him out to her car. He rubbed her crotch through her jeans, and she jerked him off into a condom, which he'd thought excessively fastidious, but didn't say, and in the moment appreciated the lubrication, and it did save on mess, so maybe she was onto something.

Cass sat up.

"Look," she said. "I don't give a fuck about Stella from Dallas. I don't think I give a fuck about any of them. But you need to keep these people out of our life. Not *my* life—*our* life. What you do out there, that's not our life."

At first it looked like he would be the one to leave. Or just the first to leave the room. He wept, overwhelmed by anger, shame, confusion—a child's reaction to feelings he doesn't understand. She consoled him, for some reason. Since they didn't have any better idea of what to do, they went back to bed. Since they didn't know how to be in bed any differently, they slid together. Since he didn't know what else to do when he held her, he kissed her earlobe, bit it gently, both their faces still wet. She turned to him in the grainy darkness, with either a half-smile of pleasure or a grimace of pity.

SUM SINE REGNO: The phone buzzed against their plywood bedframe.

Cass called him from Georgia and said she was staying at the hippie commune. Cass called him from Georgia where she was organizing voter registration. Cass called him and said she wasn't coming home. Cass said the head of the canvassing team in Savannah owned a restaurant there and needed an investor, someone who could manage the place, and that she had been saving money and that she'd just withdrawn it all. Cass said he could keep her stuff or get rid of it, it was all the same to her, that she'd had all that stuff too long anyway, that she could see the point of fires and floods that take care of that for you. Cass said that yes, she guessed she'd had him too long, too. Cass said that she didn't need a fire or flood, that it seemed like a stiff breeze would be enough to scatter him.

16

(2006-2017)

LET ME BORROW on from fortune, ran his mantra, a little more time for a poor, despicable, and wandering life.

Rudy packed his guitar and some clothes into his car, and left. What was keeping him there? What else did he have to do?

And then he simply drifted, booking himself a few weeks ahead, cycling the country in pathways interwoven like the blades of a reel mower—obsolete, but with maintenance, still roughly effective, cutting verdant life shorter with each pass.

Days and months felt like a drunk's time travel, all night or a matter of seconds. Driving past the speed of light. He became less human than refrain. His circuits eased north. Around and around and around until he just spiraled out the top.

His shows became less about the adulation of strangers than their sympathy. He could tell from the people who came up after, saying, *I wish there could've been more people, I told everyone I know, you know what, give me one of everything, yes I mean it; here, I don't need change.* Ostentatious charity. A certain kind of music fan liked their reverence to be mixed with pity, relished the spectacle of someone meeting their limitations in real time—they wouldn't have to share him, he could be their secret club. He could be idealized; maybe, romanticized, perhaps; but not respected.

He lurked around the back rooms, composing but not offering unsolicited advice—*you can back off the mic, you're blowing everybody out; lose the top-forty covers, they're pandering and needy*—for local opening acts. He allowed, from time to time, a cruel look to cross his face, meant to be noticed by the young bar staffs, meant to be received as the casual, intimidating sadism that asserts the authority of a veteran. He saw the gesture fly past its target: that guy seems like a dick, he could sense the soundman think briefly before returning to his laptop. It was easy to get a reputation as a prima donna when all he wanted was a little acknowledgment of his dignity. But the logic was implacable: if you were more popular, you'd be treated better; you don't deserve to be treated better, because nobody likes you.

He recorded a series of song collections in hotel rooms and acquaintances' basements: *Knemon. Deburau and Grimaldi.* An amateur recording of a live show from a Duluth pizza shop he called *Inkhorn Terms.* Each—like everything he, or maybe anyone, had made—was a little disappointment, a snapshot of the moment the thing passed from pure, perfect potential to imperfect existence. With everything that implied about what he was actually capable of making. Rose let him know that Bad Dream would still put out his records. Rudy refused, at first, out of a feeling that he thought of as pride, but which if he had examined it in detail would have been more accurately identified as spite.

We need a kind of VFW for old musicians, he thought, somewhere we can go and not talk to other people who don't want to talk. Even between tours, in whatever spare room was his temporary home, he sat at his computer, using Street View to wander bleak small towns, matching his mental landscape to physical ones: the empty lot behind the Hunt Brothers Pizza in Bucklin, Kansas. The Air Force base in Enid, Oklahoma. The Idle Hour in Hawthorne, Nevada. He left fantastical multiparagraph accounts of chain motels on travel sites, under the handle "Wertheimer": *My neighbors were impressive and pathetic Pninian academics, my lullabies their wall-softened Slavic consonantal abutments.*

His primary human relationship was tendentious emails to Dallin, his nominal agent, the founder and sole proprieter of Thummim Booking ("the world's only Mormon-run booking agency"). Dallin had taken on a few of Bad Dream's B-list acts as a way of currying favor with Ryan. Rudy tried to strike a balance between idly harassing Dallin (whom he'd never met, and didn't entirely think of as a real person) by way of blowing off steam and breaking the tedium, without attracting enough of Dallin's attention to make him realize that Rudy might not be worth his trouble.

Dallin—The club didn't have my name in the listing. I got three emails from people saying they had no idea I was in town.

Dallin—I went on at one in the morning, after the headliner.

Dallin—They thought it was a free show.

Dallin—The deal last night was a paper bag full of assorted coins and half a stale baguette. Where can I send your ten percent?

Dallin replied with a blithe obliviousness—*Sounds like a tough one!*—suited to a business where he would only hear from his clients when something had gone wrong. And to be fair to booking agents, Rudy thought, their jobs, like all middlemen, were easier when they didn't have to build your crowd up, or worry about your draw, and could just take the distractions of terms and contracts and payments off your hands.

There was a thin membrane between self-pitying and self-loathing, and the latter was more appealing in a performer and a person, but the former was so cozy. It wasn't personal to Dallin, or Rose or bar staff or motel keepers, or baby bands just trying to do their show. The grime and the petty humiliations matched his outer life to his inner landscape. And nourishing the sense of struggle felt honorable: if anything worth doing was hard, then anything hard was worth doing. That was just logic. Right?

HE DID FIND the drives exhilarating. The two constants in his life were, conveniently, the two places he felt most secure: on stage, and in the car. On stage, from a kind of guild pride—it was there he was exercising his skill, and doing, he felt, honest work, if a crowd let him. The car, though, had the advantage of solitude—he could exhale the burden of cordiality, the need to be solicitous of bar staff, audiences, and hosts. An all-day drive was a balm. He could let the landscape surge and swell around him, and let his mind off its leash, romp a little, gnaw and harry a notion:

Eight hours drive today, nine and a half with stops. Coffee, egg sandwich. Leave the motel card on the table, leave my stale odor in the car. Lukewarm coffee at the gas station yesterday. I complained, they offered me a complimentary box of Mike and Ikes.

Good driving game once you're off of the coasts is "public radio or Christian talk." Lose three out of four of those. Won this one. What are they talking about? Vantablack. The blackest man-made substance, swallows photons. No light, only darkness visible. Snapped up by the military, of course: mechanized killing naturally drawn to a new, darker darkness. New album title, ha, yeah I get it man, none more black, pretty fucking metal.

Nobody more sentimental than people into brutal metal and hardcore, though. Because they're committed to these utopian ideas about the way the world should behave, and they feel so personally betrayed when it lets them down. No one could be that upset unless they were a true believer. All the sentimental music, that's for the true cynics, because it's about a purity of feeling that doesn't exist in nature. It's a cliché, even, the mob hitman who goes home and puts a crooner on. Like going to a planetarium: it's so smoggy all day in the real world, it's the only way I get to see the stars. Cass said there's always light, we just pass in and out of it. No: we live in a small bubble of light in an empty universe. Darkness the natural state. Mining our souls for specks of light. Shards of joy. The sun a dull dead thing by comparison.

IT'S A KATRINA building, said the couple who put him up in New Orleans. We had to check a box on the lease saying that we knew, that we understood what that meant about the health hazards and the integrity of the structure. Anyway, it was what we could afford. The landlord went by "Shark Eyes"; we never actually met him, only talked to him on the phone. Shark Eyes had this way of both having the conversation with us, and narrating his inner monologue: "I can't come down and show it to you myself, I'm out of town. (OK, you have an interested client but you're out of town, you'll see if your friend has an extra key.) I'm going to call my friend and see if he has an extra key, OK?"

"Maybe he had a remora calling the shots," said Rudy.

He went for a walk in a wildlife refuge, a piney marsh on the north coast of Pontchartrain, laid over and sewn up by clanking, sinuous boardwalks. White cranes bobbed and fished and ignored placid-eyed gators with elegant disinterest. The wooden path dipped and splashed as he stepped, releasing puffs of brackish rot and triggering a cascade of gulps and splashes. The expectorant gulsh of a tree falling on wet ground.

He turned back when his path was blocked by a sluggish alligator. "Oh sure," said the park ranger at the front desk. "We have a couple of those. To be honest"—she lowered her voice—"I wish they'd eat those pit bulls someone let loose in the northwest part."

"Pit bulls?" said Rudy.

"Pet owners," she said, "who don't want them anymore, they let them loose in the park. They don't stand a chance. Meantime they've been chasing people around."

•••

These are the hardest roads, I-70 from Lawrence or 80 from Omaha. Straight as an iced rope, set it and forget it, but those winds southbound from Winnipeg have been picking up speed for a thousand miles. Batter the side of the car. White-knuckle it to stay straight.

Last night was one of the good ones: house show, a fireplace, a dozen people, listening, a guest room, eggs in the morning. I'm glad you're still at it, one of them said, I got the Expats stuff through a distro when I was a kid even though you never toured anywhere near me; and your songs mean the world to me. Generic but heartfelt, and I gave him a brush-off. Why? It felt good. I got that glow of affirmation. Grateful but embarrassed, then I resent that they made me feel either. Just like when my parents gave me money—ashamed of my needs, but thankful when they're met. Like that old joke: two guys fighting; one guy stops and says, why do you hate me? What did I ever do for you?

•••

HE PLAYED IN basements: carpeted American Legion basements before old men drinking, basement filth caves before black velvet curtains, brick-bellied pubs before teenage rock louts. He slept on an air mattress—were they ever comfortable?—then switched to the chaise longue, in a cozy suburban development where three post-collegiate girls sardined into a two-bedroom apartment. He slept in his car: he'd folded down the back seats to accommodate a small mattress, hung gray curtains along the windows. An empty plastic gallon for piss. The acid tang of old sweat and wool.

•••

Look at the bumper sticker. So aggressive. It's cool, I'm already Not Messing With Texas. Surely I would never.

Change the station: rock radio. An electric guitar is like looking at an American flag—some people see in it a symbol of rebellion and freedom, and some people see hegemony. The old gods snuck back in as icons and idols and lesser saints. Rock and roll was supposed to replace the church, not reincarnate it. Punk rock may not have saved as many, but it hasn't killed as many either.

But I'm too far out to swim back. The fallacy of sunk costs, I know. Music was the means—to community, camaraderie, connection—now it's not the means to anything except keeping going. I bought an all-in-one kit—a calling, an ethos, an identity—now if I tried to return it, they wouldn't take it back. Wouldn't take me back. I'm the only one still peddling a discontinued product.

The pathos of the middle-aged artist: you can flail at the panic button and start an entirely different life, or else it's long decades just hoping you stick around long enough to get "rediscovered" while you can still enjoy it. If you don't achieve escape velocity, you end up stuck in orbit, circling, speeding; can't go up, look around and realize you're crated alone, staring at the unreachable world through a passing window. If you don't flame out and crash, the only way out isn't even down.

•••

GODDAMN THIS DRIVE. *Goddamn*, this drive. Goddamn this—*drive.*

He couldn't see the elevation increasing toward Wyoming, just felt a popping of his ears every half hour, a thinning of the sky into whey-spatter clouds, and a subtle shift in the color of ground from the tan Kansan prairie to high plains lavender. He gauged his speed by the passing blood-blots of long-gone deer on the pavement; passed the I-80 high point and saw snow for the first time that year. The flag at a rest stop whipped so violently it sounded like a bonfire.

The opening act in empty Salt Lake—or was it psychotic Eugene?—was an accordionist who played seated, next to an open trash can fire. At rhythmic intervals, by way of punctuation, he threw a powder into the fire, and the flames flared past his face. Afterward, Rudy asked him what the powder was. "Nondairy creamer," he said. "It's incredibly flammable." A smear of Vaseline on his left cheek vouched for that.

Outside Sacramento on the way to the Bay, a loft party for ambitious bohemians: shaved-head entrepreneurs in white rimmed glasses who lay on pillows and low couches and looked deeply and seriously into each other's eyes, to affirm their deep seriousness. "It's so nice to have great shows," a woman enthused. "And for free!"

Skirting the cities in favor of uncontested highways and uncomplicated parking, northbound again up the rainy coast: spume on the whale-road, titanic half-calved rocks breaking the surf, fungal cliffs wet green and goldenrod under gray-scale meringues of sea cloud. Alternating patches of sunburst and shower. Soggy deserted port towns with piratical swagger. The sky full of seagulls, thick moss eroding corrugated roofs. A naval observatory clutching a boulder like a starfish. Shipping containers and tankers in bright primary colors under the menacing fog shelf. A short-tailed albatross circled and perched on the gable of a fishing-town bar. Paintings of ships hung behind the stage; candles dripped wax onto the far keys of a spinet. A tall, cylindrical wood stove nibbled a shattered heap of firewood. A ratty footstool of a bar-hound nipped Rudy on the calf with reassuring regularity every time he stepped off the stage. "Don't worry," said the owner, "he's just trying to herd you."

...

Cass in my head last night. Must be the young senator all the time on the news, the rising blue sun over the fields of red and white, triggered her memory—she'll be working for him. Years now since I saw her.

I couldn't remember the dream, but I could remember the feel of the room. The subtlety of dreams is overrated. If a dream means something, it'll be thuddingly obvious; otherwise it's just slides, the detritus of your memories gone riding.

Insistent hunger. Remember what it used to be like for vegan Cass before there was a Subway at every truck stop. French-fryitarians. Bring a bowl and some dressing and make little salads at the Roy Rogers fixings bar.

Three basic human needs: sleep, food, and sex. I'll take the one I can get.

To Carthage then I came, burning burning burning burning. (But it was cast-off Dido consumed.) Remember the girl in the blue dress in Tennessee? Seemed like there was nothing under it. There wasn't. Slim like a little boy. Sitting with her friends after the show, her leg and mine rubbing, slip my hand onto her thigh, her hand on mine. Where do we go now, she asked. How does this work? We go to one of those motels, I said. My card got declined. She put the room on hers. I'll pay you back, I said.

One hand off the wheel, rubbing through the denim. No one else on the road. Turn off the radio, I want to focus, to remember this. Blue eyes, blond finger wave. Can I? Cruise control. Pinch and pull. A rush of warmth. It'll dry. Sleepy. Pull over here.

•••

HE FORMALIZED HIS hierarchy of charity accommodations, from least to most desirable. Worst, young men living together: third-hand couches encircling video-game terminals, dishes in the sink, never-washed sheets, band posters, discount guitars with missing strings, stained toilets, unspeakable soap. Next, couples with cats, who don't think their houses smell of cat, but they've just stopped noticing. Single men living alone: a pure gamble, you could end up either at the soundman's rotting rental, huddled on a musty couch surrounded by stacks of old pornography; or a lawyer's tastefully carpeted studio—he's leaving for work early, make some coffee and hang out, take advantage of the lightning-fast internet. Married couples with children: nice places, but the household wakes at six a.m., and you're in the six-year-old's bed, under four-foot-long superhero sheets, tripping over Legos, and the kids stare at you in the morning. Best of all, childless couples over thirty: they'll have an actual guest room, the one their parents stay in when they come to visit and so has the nicest bedding they can afford. Single women living alone? Rare, and only a fool would complain.

•••

I put the cash for the room on the nightstand, I said when she got out of the shower. I only realized later how that sounded. But also it felt like that was the sort of experience she was looking for. I left her tickets for the show the next year and she showed up again, this time in a yellow dress. But I had made up with Cass by the time I got there, and I just couldn't. I looked her up on the internet later—she'd married a hippie girl and moved to Chicago. What does a hippie do in Chicago?

...

HE TURNED TOWARD the high, dry east and then into Idaho, through Snowville, Mountain Home, Twin Falls: perfectly literal, edifying names. Twin Falls was on fire: farmers were burning the fields post-harvest, and an acrid smog hung for fifty miles north of the city. Gas station attendants in neck-to-ankle Carhartt worksuits. Immense tumbleweeds piled across the road. The wind shoved him sideways.

The smoke cleared and he crossed and recrossed the Snake River, down into the valley and up onto the long tablelands, burned black on both sides of the highway. The long, low Boise suburbs slumped around mining pits and piles and putty hills.

"You come in from that way?" asked the lady at the motel check-in, thumbing east.

"Nope, the other end."

"What's it look like out there?" She took his card, swiped it, waited, punched a rubber nub. "Oh, for the love of flowers, I hit the wrong button." She swiped again.

"Just a little snow."

She shook her head. "They keep saying snow's coming, and nothing."

"Just gonna come when it comes, I guess."

"Yup." She handed him a key and turned her attention back to the high corner-mounted television.

He traveled with yards of blackout curtains carefully folded at the bottom of a suitcase. His first preparatory nesting in a fresh motel room was to light-seal the windows, gaff-taping the fabric to the irregular imitation wattle and daub. Fortifications against

insomnia. Best hope in sleep was for some of that cowboy porn—
that's what Seb used to call sex dreams—a little comfort under the
empty elements. He bathed in the low basin and watched the glum
fetid boat of a bandage floating on the tub's gray soap-scum sea.

UP AND OUT of a wide and dappled vista into the silent snow-slick
coniferous mountains, eastbound toward Missoula. The smell of
wood smoke in the air—streams of it vented from valley walls. *Ice
and snow, take it slow,* said the hazy lights of the highway sign. His
tires lost purchase each time he crossed the unplowed center lines,
and he skidded for a quarter-mile alongside a trailer hauling ceta-
cean windmill fins. A car in front of him spun and crunched into
the guardrail with a muted plastic thump. The cerulean and ivory
blur of the horizon elided the border between mountain and snow
below and clouds above. Drifts scudded in surveyor-straight channels across the road. The wind sucked an undertow between sugar-
dusted, tumorous rocks. The men at the truck stop were moai in
heavy boots, down vests over gray hoods.

He played a hangar of a sports bar, opposite a phalanx of
frozen-drink mixers windmilling hallucinatory colors labelled
Hurricane, 190 Octane, Strawberry Passion. Three men watched
NASCAR. *The cop says to me, sir, you were swerving wildly,* joked
one. *I said, I was just warming up my tires!*

Through Mile City, Montana, where a barnside mural of a
rodeo rider was captioned "Don't let meth be your last ride." A
sticker in the back window of a passing pickup proclaimed its
driver an Elkoholic. The plains, mountains, and clouds graded
blue, from deep-sea to United Nations. All the freaks of Billings
were out that night: one with Buffalo Bill beard and hair, one in
embroidered velvet tails scabbed with band pins, one in the transparent cowboy hat, and a light-blue bowtie over a T-shirt—all in

a sweating, stinking bunker with a grinning gargoyle painted over the stage. The mossy outer walls were shrouded in netting to catch concrete crumble. An unsturdy wooden balcony supported the soundman, who wheeled his gear in a stolen shopping cart. I'm not the bad kind of skinhead, he told Rudy. I'm a Trojan skinhead—I can pass. The opening act, a dapper androgyne, preened and posed.

Pancake blankness of the Dakota plain, with accents of long-haul trucking, industrial farming equipment, and desultory highway construction. A black Hummer passed, a giant decal along its side reading "Bounty Hunter." JESUS10, the license plate testified.

Rudy ate his free burger in a venue kitchen like a servant, and snuck to the stage to sound check. He slipped on some grease, landed on and snapped the headstock of his guitar. Call this number, said a bartender. He drove to a repairman's house, a retiree's garage: tools, spare parts, a glucose monitor, certificates framed and hung, a dusty unplugged rotary phone, a boom box, a space heater, stacks of LPs and periodicals. "Let's see what we've got," said the repairman, hoisting the case onto his bench and undoing the clasps. "Oof. You need it today, you said? Well, you'd better go for a walk. I'll give you a call."

"It's not a good job," he said two hours later, "but it's a quick job."

A pair of aspiring ministers took Rudy aside after the show. You have a great deal of passion, they said, and we would like to help you. They took him to a nearby park and draped their arms around his shoulders to pray for his health.

HE STAYED IN motels, disposable, all of them the same; hotels, relics, each of them different. He repeatedly awoke, in sincere

fury, to housekeepers' knocks, without ever—from an unconscious, proprietary sense of dominion—simply deigning to use
the "Do Not Disturb" sign. In a railcar room with a small sink,
the door handles were installed too close to the frame, so they
wouldn't turn all the way. Or, the doors themselves swelled so
they wouldn't close without an explosive hip check. A shower stall
down the hall; "Out of Service," said the ballpoint scrawl on the
door. Or, a shower stall in the room, but a toilet down the hall.
That's just telling you what they expect you to do.

Michigan a bleak flatland of gray and leafless trees, and a
highway patrol car every ten miles. Midnight shows on Sundays
and Mondays. "We have a late crowd here," said the bartender.
They didn't.

"Can we get you anything?" asked the promoter. "Anything
you need?"

Rudy looked at him for a long moment and shook his head
somewhere between yes and no. "I could use some fans of my
music."

17

(2006)

LAUREN HAD GOTTEN a job teaching American studies at a university in northern Virginia. She and Jules and their daughter, Lily, had a pleasant house in a pleasant neighborhood in a pleasant part of Maryland. Her aesthetic of housekeeping aspired to the level of a hotel, and Jules had gradually acquiesced.

Rudy should come for dinner and stay with them, Lauren declared, but an eleven o'clock show was past her bedtime. Jules should head in after they put Lily down, that way he could miss the openers.

Rudy watched them twirl around the kitchen in the little ballets of domesticity.

"Lily's got her three-year checkup tomorrow; can you take her, if we're gonna be up late?" Jules asked, setting forks on the table.

"Ugh," said Lauren, stirring a pot with a wooden spoon. "You're smuggling pieces of tomorrow into my beautiful today. Come here, taste this."

"What is American studies, anyway?" Rudy asked her.

"You still have no idea what I do," she said without surprise.

"Well, kids are like, oh, I'm gonna be premed, but they can't do science, so their advisors say maybe try psychology. That's still kind of medicine, right? And if they can't hack it there, they get shunted off to sociology. Then the sociology department sends them to us. You can graduate out of it basically by being born in America." She ladled sauce over plates of pasta. "Have you called Mom and Dad since they've been up in Canada?"

"Yeah, I talked to Dad. I don't think it suits him. I don't think he thought it through. He's not really a Canada person, you know? It was just a nice idea, the offer of a summer cabin. But he's not into hunting or fishing. He's not actually one of those guys who can sit alone in a cabin. He needs people to talk to. He never made any of his own friends up there. He doesn't want to impose on us—he'd never call me—but he's like a puppy dog whenever I call, he's so eager. I can't take it."

"I think that when we get annoyed with our parents as they get older, it's because it's the closest we come to seeing our future," said Lauren. "Nobody likes that. When we have these memories of them as confident and capable." Still, she added, since they'd relaxed into the role of grandparents—and after Charles's cardiac incident—they'd loosened up a little with each other as well, something closer to the way she remembered them: her father's toothy grin, her mother's unexpected cackle at a risqué joke.

Jules was six months sober, she said.

Being a musician at this age is mostly keeping track of who's quit drinking, Rudy thought. He found something a little melancholy about his friends who got clean. You catch people in bad light, or too early, or in new, thicker glasses, and you get a flash of what they'll look like when they're old. New sobriety was something like that. You're happy for them, of course, and they get their cheekbones back, but some of the vitality goes out of them.

Shrunken versions of themselves, physically, but also without that widescreen emotional range. Some of them went gray: the tension of playing watchman to themselves.

"Had to," Jules said, later, Lauren long since gone to bed. Jules took a seltzer with bitters ("I call this a Cold Turkey," he said) and Rudy a red wine to the back deck. "I was dancin' with the deuce. Two hundge ain't a good look on a guy my size."

"Yeah, jeez. What'd you do with the rest of you."

"Easy the first time, they say. You get a thirty pound bonus for joining." Jules kicked a pink soccer ball away from the latticed iron table. "I used to quit for Lent every year. Just to make sure, you know? You ever try that?"

"Just this year," said Rudy. "For Lent, I gave up. That feels good too."

"Oh, boo-hoo. Life you chose. You can stop, you know. I did."

"Hell would I do with myself all day? Who's gonna hire me? I don't want to tend bar for the rest of my life. I've got a sinkhole in my CV at this point. A town-swallower."

"Well, yeah," said Jules. "You have to start over. I'm not saying it was easy. Everyone my age was ten, fifteen years deep into their careers when Lily was born, becoming managers and principals and tenured professors and department heads. It's not like you can get entry-level jobs at thirty-whatever. We'd just moved up here, didn't know anyone. I learned you shouldn't get drunk in a new town. People think that's what you're like." He crossed his legs at the knee. "You know how hard it is to make friends as a grown person? People already *got* friends, they're not looking for new ones. I'd meet someone I thought was cool at a kid's birthday, and it was all I could do to not act like a freak, keep mentioning, like, hey man, let's hang out sometime. And they always ask what you do—fair question, of course, they're just being polite. I used to be able to say 'musician.' I was proud of it. People thought that was cool, they had questions, maybe they even had an Expats seven-inch when they were in college. Now—what? Stay-at-home dad? People respect that in theory. But I always feel like it's still code for unemployed loser. Probably I'm projecting. Having kids dilutes your ego, it doesn't dissolve it. But Lauren has a built-in social circle, she's the new professor, they come over and talk work and babies."

"Moms at the playground?" Rudy offered.

"I can't crack 'em. I'm telling you, everyone's a little suspicious of dads. Anyway, it's babies all the way down with them—who's a picky eater, who's got a new sitter. I was with Lily all day at that point. Last thing I wanted to talk about. But the moms, they made it seem like this was the life they'd been working toward. Stretch pants and easy authority. I've never known how to talk to someone who's not missing something in their lives."

"You sure they're not."

"Point is you can't tell."

Rudy swirled his wine. A security light clicked on over the neighbor's garage. "Lauren said you're trying for another, though."

"Yeah, going from zone defense to man-to-man." Jules snorted. "Least this way I get to have sex with my wife again. Sorry, I know that's your sister."

"None taken." The more their lives had diverged, the less he thought of Lauren as a sister in the way he had when they were younger, that mixture of intimacy and competitiveness. Their parents' ingenuous openness had manifested in Rudy and Lauren as a brutal, mutual candor.

"Plus," Jules said, "we oughta give Lily someone to play with. I'm her go-to playmate right now, and that's not ideal for either of us." He sighed. "There are all these stock phrases people use to talk about having kids, 'It's not about you anymore' and all that. Meaningless. It's like you've passed the event horizon: you can make all these plans, but you don't know what it's going to be like afterward, and people who've gotten there can't send any information back."

Jules refilled their glasses. "Babies are fucking boring. I feel like one of those African villagers who squat for days waiting for a bus. Or a prisoner composing a novel in his head. You start to understand all these old jokey clichés, like how for Father's Day what dad really wants is a six-pack and to be left alone—to have a break from being a father. But what I really have is a whole new empathy for that classic housewife. All I do is cook, wash dishes, change diapers, go shopping, drive Lauren and Lily places, try to keep from day drinking. I'm Betty fuckin' Friedan. But nobody sheds any tears for the plight of the stay-at-home dad, women have been doing this for all of human history, I get it. Why moms get so insistent about their special diets and their self-help spirituality tapes—anything to put stakes up to protect their identities."

How did fathers do it? Alcohol and furtive masturbation, Rudy supposed. Sex life over and done by forty. Easier, anyway. Let go of that peacock urge and slip through life as unnoticed as possible. For Jules, it seemed, becoming a parent had been something like being out for a walk and getting splashed by an oncoming car: unexpected, unpleasant, but you dry eventually, and in any case most of the mud got on his wife.

"Here's the funny thing," Jules continued. "I think I'm pretty *good* at it. I was talking to the wife of one of Lauren's colleagues. We'd had a few drinks and I was getting at some of these like mixed feelings, and she couldn't believe it. 'You seem like such a devoted dad,' she said. 'I assumed it'd been something you'd always wanted.' And my joke was—not even a joke, really—that the kid was a good excuse to leave a party. If she started complaining or getting bored or needed a diaper, I got to split and get credit for being a superdad.

"But I tell you what—last year or so, I'm starting to think, and maybe I'm just giving in to it, but I'm starting to think it is something I want. Or at least I want it now. Maybe you just need something to knock yourself outside your life, get some perspective. Calm the fuck down. The last year, now she's talking, has · her own weird ideas, we can have little conversations about what she's thinking about, whether chipmunks eat people, why when you pour salt on wet watercolors it makes little stars, which colors are in the evil rainbow. You know what she did the other day? She came up behind me on the couch, put her hands on my shoulders, and whispered in my ear: 'You had a good run.' She meant I went jogging. Still terrifying. True, too, though."

Jules had gone hugely, geologically bald. Moonlight gleamed off his newly dignified forehead. "Plus she's going to have to answer for my life, and I'm going to have to answer to her for it. You can play at nihilism, or masochism, when it's just you and you don't care that much about yourself, because you already don't think that much of yourself. No one will ever say about me, 'He never hurt anyone.' Too late for that. But we 'practice' restraint, right? Like you practice an instrument, in fits and starts, because someone tells you to, grudgingly, badly, not getting it right and then getting better. It'll be a hell of a lot easier for me from now on if I can just leave out doing the wrong things."

Rudy had never heard Jules talk with this depth of feeling and self-awareness, of which, fairly or not, he hadn't thought Jules capable. It hadn't occurred to him that people who took the opportunity for a comfortable life had made not just a practical decision for themselves, but a moral one.

"Let me put it this way," Jules said. "I got carpal tunnel from doing data entry at my last temp job, and it's been hard to play guitar anyway. Let's say aging is about the slow acquisition and then the slow loss of control: I learn to control my hands, and then use my hands to control the world; then eventually I lose control of my hands, and then I lose control of the world around me. Children, the same: I shape them, briefly, and then they're lost to me."

"The arc of competence," said Rudy. "When you're a kid, you don't know shit, you can't do shit. When you're a young person, you can do shit, but you don't know shit. A grown-up, you know shit and you can do shit. A good feeling, even if it's a bad time. Then—and you don't even know when it happens—you know shit, but you can't do shit."

"You shape your songs," Jules said. "You put them out into the world, and then what are they to you? You don't have to keep watching over them year after year. You don't have any idea what their lives are like. They have their own relationships, with people you'll never meet. Our ideas about our lives are a trick of the mind. Some people look in a puddle and see the sky, some see themselves, some see nothing but mud."

Jules got up. "Maybe it's not where I would've chosen," he said, "but I decided to bloom where I'm planted. Let's call it. Lily's probably gonna come jump on you earlier than you want. Plus I've got it on good authority that looking backwards gets you pillar of salt. I better step lightly for a while."

18

"ONE, TWO, FREE, *four, monsters walking out the door. I love counting, counting to the number four.* Uno, dos, tres, cuat—cuarto? Oh! I will do it again. Tres, cuatro, cinco, seis. Oh! My dolly needs a new diaper. I'm the big sister. I'm gonna change her diaper. Dada, where's my dolly's stripy blanket? She's crying. She needs her pacifier. Now she feels better. Can you help me snap the new diaper? Oh thank you. Dada, where's mama? How come mama's not here? How come mama's at work? Can you read a book to me? I want you to read the alligator book to me. Friends with an alligator! I wouldn't want to be friends with an alligator. Lunch with an alligator! The alligator wants to eat you for lunch. Dada can you sit up? Why you want to stay in bed? I want you to read these books to me. But I want you to read all of them! Where's Fish the Bear? Where's Coconut? Where's Flat Monkey? Dada who's sleeping on the couch in the office? Uncle Rudy? How come Uncle Rudy is sleeping on the couch? What's a guest? When Grandpa Charles comes he sleeps in the office. How come that's where guests sleep? Why we have to be quiet? Can I wake up Uncle Rudy? Why he wants to keep sleeping? Why he doesn't feel well? I'm the doctor. I will give him some medicine. Check your heart. Check your ears. Say aah. You need to go to the hospital, dolly. She wants her stripy blanket. She wants her pacifier. Oh! Now she feels better."

Rudy rolled over, springs and joints creaking, on the foldout couch. He pressed his face against the twill as Lily's monologue, and Jules's muffled interjections, floated to the surface of his awareness. Sunlight spilled around roller shades. The tiny bongo slaps of toddler footsteps crescendoed from the master bedroom to Jules's home office. Rudy turned back, and found himself inches from Lily's blithe, curious face.

"Can we brush teeth?" she asked, in a cracked meow. "I want to brush my teeth with you."

"Good morning to you, too," said Rudy. "And who is your friend?"

Lily held out, with two stiff arms, a plush creature with a stuffed head and unstuffed body. "This is Flat Monkey."

"Hello, Flat Monkey." Rudy shook its limp paw. "Now that you mention it, I could stand to brush my teeth, thank you for asking. Does Flat Monkey brush his teeth?"

Lily cackled. "He doesn't have *teeth!*"

"Of course not," said Rudy. "My mistake. Can you show me where the bathroom is?"

"Yes," she said definitively, and scurried out the door in a flash of pink and white pajamas. He groaned upright and followed, belly proofing over gray boxers.

Lily was waiting, with a proprietary hand on a folded two-step stool, to walk her new assistant through her routine. "I need my step. Thank you. I need a gummy vitamin. Can you unscrew that for me? No, I want a yellow one! That's an orange one! I want to spread the toothpaste! Oh thank you. Look, I can spit! Ptuh. Can I have some water? No, I wanna wash it off. I want to go downstairs. I want my slippers. I want to wear my robe. Why you don't have a robe?"

"Exposed to the world's contempt. You're right, a robe would be nice."

"You can borrow my dad's robe. Otherwise you would be *naked*!" She cackled again.

"I think he's already wearing it." Rudy cupped his hand theatrically behind his ear. "I hear him in the kitchen."

Lily considered this. "OK, you come downstairs when you get dressed. I will go first."

She descended the stairs carefully, right hand on a banister higher than her head. Flat Monkey lay forsaken on the tiled floor; Rudy set it hunkered on a green plastic frog potty. While he dressed, Rudy heard Lily negotiating with Jules: "I don't want oatmeal, I want pancakes! I want to help! I need my steps. Can you open this for me? No I wanna scoop the coffee. One . . . two . . . free . . . four. Four scoops! Wait, I wanna push the button." She sang to herself while the coffee ground: "*One, two, free, four, monsters coming back for more.* I don't like coffee. Yucky coffee! Kids don't like food that's yucky. Only grownups like food that's yucky. I would like a peanut butter and jelly for lunch. Would you like a peanut butter and *smelly* for lunch? Ha ha! Did you ever hear of a peanut butter and smelly?"

Rudy nodded good morning to Jules, who presented an open hand to the scene in the kitchen by way of saying, you see what it's like around here.

"Uncle Rudy, do you like pancakes? I want to tell you the in—in—in—ingredients! First you break the egg. I want you to break the egg. No I want to do the whisk! Ooh cottage cheese! One. Two. Free. But I want to do one more! Oh yes, I will eat one. Four. Flour comes next! One. Two. Uh-oh, I spilled some! Big mess! Hey wait, you forgot the vanilla. Just a little bit! I need to get down. Can you help me get down?"

He picked her up under her armpits and swung her to the floor, her bare feet flapping, already running to the other room before they'd touched down. "OK dolly, I'm the mama and you're the baby and you need a new diaper. Waah! She's crying. Don't worry baby, I will give you a new diaper. Wipe, wipe. Ooh, stinky! Put it in the garbage. You have to say thank you! Now you are all clean. Naptime, naptime. I will tuck you in. Only two stories, baby. I will sing you a song. *All the bridges falling down, falling down, falling down, all the bridges falling down, my fair lady.* Dada, can I tell you something? My dollies are sleeping! We have to be quiet. Oh! Now they are awake! Dada, can we go on a walk? I will push my baby in a stroller."

"Not yet, sweetie," said Jules. "Wait for the pancakes to be ready. Do you want to draw?"

"Yeah I want to draw!" She scampered back in to the kitchen and clambered up onto a chair at the table. "I need some paper. No, fresh paper! Markers, markers, markers. Draw, draw, draw. I made a card for Uncle Rudy. It's a red sun, and a yellow sun, and a blue sun, and a green sun, and a purple sun. Red and blue make purple! Can you fold it for me? Now we need to staple it."

"The stapler's in my desk, in the office," said Jules.

"Why the stapler is in your desk?"

"That's where it belongs."

She climbed back down from the table and ran upstairs. "No running with the stapler!" Jules yelled, without conviction. He looked at Rudy. "How'd you sleep?"

"Coulda been longer," said Rudy, "but you can't beat the wake-up call."

Jules laughed. "That's what I mean," he said. "Even if she keeps me up all night, it's hard to stay upset. After all, I did this to myself. The hedonists were wrong. Self-inflicted misery, at least you feel like you've got some control over it." He flipped the pancakes, called upstairs: "Lily! Breakfast!"

Lily reappeared, an open Swingline dangling from her hand. "I want pancakes! I want four pancakes! I want them on the airplane plate! Don't spread the syrup around please! I want milk please! In the stripy cup. With a bendy straw. A green bendy straw!" She stuffed a piece of pancake in her mouth. "Ow, too hot! Can you blow on them for me? I want you to blow on them! Ooh, yummy pancakes. Dada, I have four pancakes! One. Two. Free. Four. When my baby brother comes, we're going to be four in the family. I'm gonna be the big sister. When my baby brother comes home, he can sleep in my room. Uncle Rudy can sleep in the office. Is he gonna sleep in my old crib? Can we have a bunk bed when he gets bigger? I will use the ladder. Dada, who is Uncle Rudy's mama? Who is Uncle Rudy's dada? Mama is Uncle Rudy's sister! Ha ha! That's funny." Temporarily sated, she stapled all four corners of the folded paper, pressing with both hands and a small effortful grunt, and presented the result to Rudy.

He turned it over in his hands. "How will I open it?" he asked.

"You don't open it. It's a secret." She pushed her plate away. "All done! Can you get me down? Thank you. Dada, I want to go to the playground."

"We can't go to the playground right now," said Jules, "we have a guest."

"I don't want to go to the playground with you, I want to go to the playground with Uncle Rudy. Uncle Rudy, can you go to the playground with me?"

Rudy looked at Jules, who shrugged. "Sure, I'll take you to the playground."

"Yay!" She pulled him out the front door. "I want to take my scooter! I can snap the helmet. I don't want you to pinch me. Whee! Look I can use the brake so I don't go into the street. We don't want to get hit by a car! That would be a big boo-boo. *Row,*

row, row your boat, gently down the drain. Merrily merrily merrily merrily, life is bottle dream. Do you know that song? Why you live that song? I want to go on the big-girl swing. Can you give me a underdog? Look I'm going so high! Uncle Rudy can I tell you something? For my birthday I had raspberry cake. Next year I will be four. For my next birthday I want blueberry cake. I want shmooberry slake? Ha ha! Did you ever hear of kloomery crake? Ha ha! When my baby brother comes he won't know how to talk or use the potty and I will show him. I want to go on the yellow slide. You come with me. We're on a train to the city. I'm the conductor. You say 'Are we at the city yet?' No, person, we're not at the city yet. OK conductor, you say. 'We're here!' I'm going to visit my cousins. They have good toys, right? Uncle Rudy, do you have cousins? Is Mama your sister? Are you a dada? Why you're not a dada? Why it just didn't happen? Why everyone's better off?"

"I'm not always good at playing with other people like you are."

"Well, I like to play with you anyway. Oh! My dolly wants to go on the swing! Ha ha she fell off! Why it's time to go home? Ooh the sidewalk is so bumpy! Can you stay with me tonight? Why you have to keep driving? Dada, I want Uncle Rudy to stay with me tonight and read me two books. Why it's not his turn? Why Uncle Rudy has to go?"

19

EVERY THIRD SEASON, Rudy took a month or two off: he needed to be a recluse for a while after a long stretch of tour, needed to shut a door behind him and refresh his capacity for dealing with people. Come back too quick, you get the bends. Gotta spend some time in the chamber.

He alighted in a college town, a station town, in upstate New York. He rented a small A-frame; a mail-order house, from the turn of the twentieth century. The original landlords had ordered it from the Sears catalog, and a truck pulled up at the lot with all the precut parts; each board, each nail delivered machine-chiseled and beveled—the workingman's dream home, and wasn't he a workingman? The great joke of the prefab in an artisanal age was that without the vagaries of individual local carpenters, the off-the-rack houses were tight and lasted a hundred years. Soft pine floors that dented under metal chair legs, the creaks and clanks at night, a little droop in the ceilings, mice, some lost young bats who took a wrong turn out of the attic learning to fly, an annual swarm of acrobat ants to vacuum up—perfectly fine.

A station town bred grouchy natives: the hooting late-night whistles, the bloom of parking regulations, the late commuters barreling heedless down the small Main Street. There was, though, a pub on the corner. The owner, Jozef, was two generations removed from Poland, and beginning to leather and mummify with cigarettes. He was lean, and unexpectedly muscular when he stripped off his shirt to work on the fence. (He had to add a few feet—the college kids were passing bottles over it from the adjoining alley.) He slept in an apartment above the bar, behind an American flag curtain. He knocked on Rudy's door and introduced himself, a courtesy to a new neighbor: "I wanted to give you my number. You call me if there's ever a problem with the noise."

Rudy liked to think of himself as the kind of guy who could live by a bar, even wanted to. But those Thursday night college dance parties, student DJs, the dull mallet thud of the kick drum—if you live in a city, everyone comes across as basically about twenty-seven, so you don't notice you're older until you live in a place where adults and kids exist as separate kinds of being. People used to sleep in two shifts, up for an hour or two to read, write, have sex; and Rudy supported reviving old practices in theory, but it seemed like a waste of the concept to lie awake fuming. Both etiquette and the law, he felt, were on his side. He went to see Jozef every Friday morning for five weeks to complain. He took early morning weekend walks, picking beer bottles off the lawns and sidewalks.

On the sixth Friday, Rudy slept through the night. In the morning, he sat drinking coffee on his porch. Jozef was carrying a piece of corrugated tin to his truck. He put it down and walked over. "Any noise last night?"

"I guess not, seemed fine."

"Good," said Jozef. "I think I've got it taken care of."

"What'd you do?" Rudy set his mug on a small ceramic table.

"I turned the fuckin' bass all the way down. Then I pulled

off the knob and squirted Krazy glue all over it. That little fucker won't move again no matter what the kids try to do."

Jozef's methods were crude, but, Rudy had to admit, effective.

"Mind if I smoke?" Jozef asked, pulling a pack of cigarettes from his shirt pocket.

"Would it matter if I said yes? I find it usually doesn't."

"Hey, OK, gear down, big rig." He smacked the cigarettes back. "Listen, you ever tended bar?"

"It's been a while," said Rudy. He'd been a dishwasher one summer as a teenager, came back the next year as a busboy. On his second night, the restaurant got busy, and the manager told him to get behind the bar to help out. He was seventeen, not that anyone asked, and he hadn't had more than a few beers in his life at that point. The first guy who ordered asked for a gin and tonic. Rudy sidled over to the other bartender and asked him what was in a gin and tonic. Well, he said. You got your gin. And then you got your tonic.

"We just had someone quit," Jozef said. "Come in Wednesday around five. See what you remember."

LAUREN WAS boycotting him.

A heart attack and subsequent surgeries—the works, he said, they gave me the works—had forced Charles into what he considered early retirement. (He hadn't much considered retirement at all.) This, in turn, sent Olivia back to work, in the office at the local elementary school. They'd always put their whims and their children, usually in that order, over their finances, and trusted in what they wouldn't have called providence. Their plans, to the extent they had them, focused more on ends than means. Now, with Charles's lengthy convalescence and uncertain recovery, those ends—travel, light writing—receded. Olivia called Lauren and asked her to come to Madison. Lauren, in turn, called Rudy: Mom needs help. I have a young child, a full-time job, and a tenure book to revise. You have—what do you have, exactly?

Rudy refused. A thirty-seven-year-old man, moving back in with his parents? He'd feel like a failure. He'd look like a failure. They'd receive him without judgment, the parents who had told him he could do anything he set his mind to. Perhaps he blamed them, in a childish way, when that had been proven false. Anyway, it was intolerable.

"You're misinterpreting, or misunderstanding, the situation," Lauren said. "Whether you're doing that on purpose, I can't tell. Going home to take care of a sick parent isn't the same thing as you dropped out of college and can't find a job."

"Either way, I'm living in the basement," he said. "It's not the kind of thing I'm good at."

"It's the kind of thing you have to do whether you're good at it or not!" she yelled, and hung up. She was able to arrange a semester's unpaid leave, and flew to Madison, staying in Charles and Olivia's basement guestroom through spring and summer. Since she and Rudy, it became clear, had only spoken when she called him, they didn't for a while.

INSTEAD, HE GOT a rambling email now and then from Jules. It would start with a perfunctory, though not insincere, inquiry after Rudy—*Hey Rude. Just checking in to see how country living suits you*—before pivoting to Jules's discursive ruminations on the course of his life, which was static in a way that allowed him to grumble about it without threatening its comfortable predictability. *Walking around campus next to my daughter on her hand-me-down princess bike, which she begged for and loves by the way, getting dirty looks from young men in dresses. Like I'm actively trying to prop up the patriarchy. Motherfucker, you don't know me.* The failure of Lauren's pregnancy had been agonizing; and, for a while, they'd abandoned the idea of more children. Jules had eventually gone to work as an account manager at a local ad agency. *I heard from Seb recently—did you know he's trying to put together a new Expats? He asked what I was up to, did I want to play. He can't quite imagine how different my life is, since he hasn't let his change at all. I mean, we were popular enough that people were sad when we broke up, but not enough that they're clamoring for us to return. Everyone who liked us is our age, you know? I guess he thinks he can put together the world's best Expats cover band and no one will notice. He's probably right about that, just not in the way he thinks.* Rudy hadn't talked to Seb in, what, seven, eight years? Playing his nonhits with a band half his age—it was a door to keep closed. Though, how different was it from what he was doing. There you had it, anyway, the descent of an idea, look what it had wrought: Seb, abject; Rudy, desperate; Ryan—well, for Ryan, it had worked. But Ryan would have been a success even if I'd never met him. The world likes Ryans.

He hadn't talked to Cass in almost as long either, come to think of it. Funny how people just disappear from your life, if you don't go out of your way to keep them in it.

Anyway I wanted to send you something Lily did at school, I thought you'd get a kick out of it. The assignment was to write about someone famous, and guess who she picked? Ha ha. Anyway, talk soon, hope you're well. J.

Lily Chance

Ms. Morton's class

Summer Bird Elementary School

My Uncle Rudy plays music. He is famous because people who are strangers know his name, but I don't think he is rich and famous. I asked him did he make a lot of money and he said no, and I asked him did he want to and he said only because if you have money people don't bother you as much. I heard some of Uncle Rudy's songs and I didn't understand what they were about. I asked him what his songs were about and that was the only time he didn't answer me. One time when he stayed at our house, he showed me how he has a bed and a pillow in the back of his car so he can sleep there. It was like my pillow fort I make with stuffed animals and do stories with them. It looked fun to sleep in a car, because then you could just drive anywhere and you would always have a home, because you brought your home with you like a turtle. I wonder if he misses his family? I love my mom and dad but also I want to run away sometimes too. So I think Uncle Rudy must be happy.

The door of the pub swung open. A pair of thick black eyebrows yawed in. Not the walk of a man who was drunk already, but one whose muscle memory has him halfway there. "You have Genesee?" he asked Rudy. He turned his head and yelled. "Hey Jozef! Have you always had Genesee?"

"Leon, are you kidding?" Jozef replied. "That's all you've ever ordered when you come in here."

A regular, then. Leon pulled out a stool. Rudy pulled a draft and set it in on the bar.

"Oh, man." Leon pointed at a half-empty highball glass waiting to be cleared. "Make me something like that. With citrus and fruit. What is that?"

"It's—like a cosmo," Rudy said.

"Give me the leftovers, I want to taste it."

Rudy dumped the dregs in a tumbler, and shoved it Leon's way.

Leon sniffed at the glass, then emptied it into his beer. "Call it a Fruity Jenny. I love this shit." He waved at the one college kid getting a head start on his night. "Remember, I bought you two pitchers of melonballs for your birthday?" He got a nod and a raised glass in return. "You and the mayor! The mayor, he drinks here."

Jozef woke the laptop that drove the bar's music. He poked around in a playlist labeled "polack tracks."

"You live around here?" Rudy asked Leon.

"I'm a janitor for municipal transport, twenty-five years. Wiping down buses in the yard. I'm fifty, I can retire in five years. I live in a homeless tent in the city. Tent Two. Tent One is my best friend, Bogey Dick Itch. He's Serbian. He's from Belgrade. He's sixty-six. I've got a nice tent. All the girls want to stay there. But I don't touch them. They all say, Leon, he's a gentleman, he never tries anything. I found this one girl walking in the park one night in a bikini and no shoes. I gave her my sneakers and let her stay in my tent. Anything coulda happened to her. She kissed me, I didn't do nothing."

Jozef grabbed two pint glasses and twisted them upside down over the conifer brushes, sloshed them in the disinfectant. "He got screwed over by this chick he was involved with," he said quietly to Rudy. "He was pretty frugal, you know, he likes to have a drink, but he had a house and everything. She took him for eighty grand. He lost his house and he can't get anything to rent, so he lives in a tent. Comes up here once a month, like a vacation. God, I love him. If I had a bar full of people like him, I'd be happy."

THAT NIGHT, UNEXPECTEDLY, he got an email from Lily herself—lilyofthealley@gmail.com, no subject:

Hi Uncle Rudy. My dad told me he sent you the paper I wrote for Ms. Morton's class, and I was mad at him, because I can write you an email myself, like this. How are you? Are going to come stay with us again soon?

I'll tell you some things about my life. I like my school, even though today Amelia, when we were lining up with our backpacks, went and pulled everyone's strap off their shoulder, just one strap and not the other. She said you should only wear your backpack with one strap. I like wearing my backpack with both straps, because that way I can see how the glitter design on one side is the opposite of the glitter design on the other side, but she said no. So that was a bad thing that happened today. I will write a good thing and a bad thing that happened. A good thing that happened today was I got a new book from the library. I read a lot of books, like one every week. I like thinking about how everything could be totally different from what it looks like and my house could be a secret powerful place and not just a regular house with a backyard and I could be super powerful and fight evil. Also, we have crows in our neighborhood.

I think a lot about things that are fair and not fair. Like Miss Morton said the temperatures are rising and the ocean is rising and it's because we don't pay attention to what we use and that's not fair. Why do some people use more things than they need if it's going to kill animals and stuff? I asked Mom if we could get solar panels for our house and she said maybe. I already ride my bike everywhere, so that's good. Also there are people who are sleeping in the park downtown, and they made signs and are shouting because they are mad because some people have a lot of money and some people don't have any. I think people should share their money if they have a lot. My dad said they tried that and it wasn't good, but maybe they didn't do it right. I told Miss Morton about the people in the park and she said we could start a book club, just the two of us. She said we could call it Morton's Academy for Dissenters, and I said what's a dissenter and she said I was.

I forgot to tell you Miss Morton has black boots and she has a tattoo that is coming out of the back of her boots, but I don't know what it is, though; it's just a design. I like to look at that while we read, and she has black hair that looks like a helmet kind of.

So Miss Morton and me are reading the Odyssey, which you say "Odesee," just the two of us, and in it Odysseus travels around and he has lots of adventures, but he is trying to get home. I told her my Uncle Rudy also travels around a lot and has adventures. But I don't know if he is trying to get home. Also Odysseus in the book lies a lot and tricks people, and I don't think Uncle Rudy lies a lot and tricks people. Like when I ask him a question he answers it and doesn't say maybe or I'll tell you later.

Well I hope you come stay with us again soon. Will you?

Love, Lily

He wrote back with a joke—*I will, but I'll tell you later when*—and their epistolary exchange continued, erratic but unbroken, a comforting medley of anecdote, gossip, and advice, until the distractions of middle school drew Lily away. Rudy hadn't, in fact, gotten around to visiting in some time, and he understood that to Lily he was a kind of harmless abstraction, a Dear Diary who wrote back. He printed out her more substantial letters and kept them in a folder in his guitar case. From Jules's sporadic parallel notes, it was clear that she hadn't told her parents she was in touch—an innocuous omission more than an evasion, and he kept her secret for his own reasons: he valued the cozy certainty of their correspondence, and the easy freedom he felt to tell her about his life. After all, who else did he have?

IT WAS LIKE some kind of mating ritual for the college kids, a girl standing by in her pajama sweatpants on a frigid morning while a guy dug out her Ford Focus. Getting shoveled out—sounds dirty. The whirring of wheels spinning frictionless in the snow. They all came in the bar on Thursdays, speaking fluently the languages of recovery, the DSM-5, and graduate-level gender studies. This one, with a smoker's voice and a drinker's slur, putting five old-fashioneds on a credit card. That one, plain, with childishly stubby nails and penetrating eyes, the kind of girl who gets invited to dinner with professors, and ends up with a sub rosa junior-faculty boyfriend.

Rudy's best friend in high school had been one of these types, a slim redhead with thin lips, sexually precocious in a mousy and self-contained way. Their group of friends all knew the six students she'd slept with, that there was one more, and that she wouldn't say who—the physics teacher, was the theory, the athletic one with the push-broom moustache. Finally, in Rudy's third or fourth year of being in love with her, sitting on the wooden benches in the student lounge, she asked Rudy, "Do you want to kiss me?" Just asked, out of nowhere, as if to test a theory. Their teeth clicked, lips limp, and it was over. They walked to the gym. "Do you think—can I get another chance at that?" he asked, as they passed the baseball field. "No," she said. "I found out what I needed to know."

The DJ—LA kid, half-buttoned shirt—introduced himself chummily, ordered the first of his string of free drinks, plugged in his laptop. Rudy tore up a napkin, rolled the strips into flimsy pills, and stuffed one in each ear canal.

A guy in an orange hunter's vest ordered a White Russian,

pulled a bottle of Yoo-hoo from his pocket, asked, "Can you make it with this?"

A procession of whiskey sours. Extra cherries please.

Seven tequila shots spilled, *shit, fuck, lemme get seven more.*

"You're done," Rudy said, and mopped up.

As the distraught student launched into an apologia and a negotiation, Jozef eased over with a rag to help Rudy clear the mess. A smog of noise enveloped the pub, but something—the hanging stemware, perhaps—blocked enough frequencies to scrub a bubble of clear quiet behind the bar. "Listen," Jozef said to Rudy. "I don't want to undercut your authority. If you cut her off, I'm gonna back you up." He swept a palmful of lime wedges into the trash. "But let me tell you something. When I first moved to this country, I worked at a cop and fireman bar in the outer boroughs, a real bucket-of-blood place. The firemen, I liked—anyone who runs into a burning building is my kind of guy. The cops were sour little pricks, with their stingy-ass Budweisers. There were a lot of Irish in the neighborhood, but the biggest ethnic group was Scandinavians—Swedes and Norwegians. They were rough. If your pour was just a titch light, they would let you have it."

He stacked the seven shot glasses in the corner of the sink. "We had this one lady, I called her the Mimosa Queen. She would come in around eleven in the morning, hair done up, makeup perfect—by midafternoon she'd be a mess. And this guy Frank, he'd drink a bottle and a half of Dewar's every day. He'd fucked up his life, his kids wouldn't talk to him. Silver hair in a pompadour. I said to him one day, 'Frank, you know, you're drinking too much.' The bar manager called me over and started yelling at me: 'If you ever do that again I'll fucking tear you apart. I don't care if you have to pour it down his throat with a funnel!'"

He gathered a pile of cardboard coasters in one palm, looked at them, threw two, soggy and ripped, away, and placed the rest neatly back in the caddy with the cocktail straws. "That's what you get paid for as a bartender—not for dealing with people who know how to act in a bar. Hundreds of good people come here to take a break from being good people, so you get paid to take a break from judging them."

He ran a rag over the brass taps. "The students, they're like another species that live among us. They're just playing, trying lives on; they'll leave in a year or two, never think of us again. But Thursday night pays the rent." He threw a handful of bottles into the recycling bin. "The old owner, when the bar looked like it was gonna be foreclosed, he separated every item into labeled file drawers—zesters, juicers, strainers, coasters—and wrote a complete accounting on a legal pad. Made it as easy as possible to assess." He looked at Rudy. "You know, he quit drinking the day he sold me this place."

part V

20

(2018)

LILY WAS SITTING on a park bench reading a zine with a degraded black-and-white cover. The text was handwritten in a neat sans serif all-caps. Next to her was a crumpled green army bag, a half-collapsed yawning dumpling. She was wearing a very short black denim skirt, and her pale legs were covered in bruises down to the point where they were swallowed by oversized black boots. She wore a grimy black sweatshirt with a hood over a fraying dyed-black bob. Her lips glared red.

"This," she said when she saw Rudy. She shook the book at him, or at the sky. "Before you ask, I was looking for this. Just to jump on a bus and go and find shitty coffee and old thrift shops and, I don't know, sit in a drainage pipe with some weirdo kid. Shoplift cereal and, like, run a receipt scam. Find some temporary friends and sleep on their floor. I'm not mad at Mom. Dad is whatever, he's Dad. Nothing's wrong at school. I just wanted to leave."

She had a high, creaking voice. No one takes me seriously, she said, because I sound like an elementary schooler. She'd been gone a month, she told him. "Mom just about shit kittens when I called from Davenport. Did you know Quad Cities is actually five cities?"

"I've gotta call Lauren," he said.

"Don't call Mom," she said. "I'm not a runaway. I'm not running away. I'm just done there. I want to come with you for a while. I can sell your merch."

"How did you get here?"

"Buses. I had money from babysitting last summer. I got as far as Minneapolis and it was gonna run out. I didn't know where else to go. I saw you were gonna be here, so I spent the rest on the ticket. It took for fucking ever and nothing interesting happened. The bus smelled like a toilet. Can I take a nap in your car?"

SHE WAS ALREADY asleep, curled on his humid mattress, as he pulled the curtains closed. He called his sister.

"Oh my God, Rudy. Is she OK?"

"Good to talk to you, too. Long time."

"Cut the shit, Rudy. How is my daughter?"

"Seems fine. It's like it didn't even touch her. She sailed across the country just kind of grouchy that it didn't reach out and grab her. She's tired and needs a shower and a burger."

"Jesus Christ. Put her on."

"Let the kid sleep."

There was a pause on the line and a muffled choking sound, then the high keening of a child in distress.

"This is what being a parent is, Rudy," Lauren said, finally. "One child disappears across the fucking country, doing God knows what. Meanwhile the other is throwing a fit because he wants his grilled cheese cut in four pieces instead of two. And I gotta take them both equally seriously."

"I'll take care of her," he said. Prefab language filling the awkward pause.

"You'll take care of her. Like you took care of Dad? Did you know he was back in the hospital? Did you know I've been flying out there every weekend? Did you even know Lily was missing? We've been in a crisis over here and you're, what, watching trees go by and counting your grievances?"

This time he let the pause be.

"How soon can you get her here?" Lauren said, in a lower tone. "I'd say put her on a plane, but I want eyes on her all the way to my door."

"I'm heading that way. I've got shows in Billings and Iowa City. A week? Ten days?"

"A week. Please. And Rudy, get hotel rooms. I don't need my daughter living like a vagrant any more than she already has. She sleeps in the car with you, she'll get the idea that it's easy. Forget that she's got an adult there keeping an eye on her who fucking bought the car and pays for the gas and car insurance. I'll send you the money if you need it."

"I don't need it."

"Rudy."

"Yeah."

"How many drinks do you have before you leave the club?"

"I can get her to a hotel."

"You can?"

"I am capable of the basic levels of responsibility."

She laughed, finally. "Thank you, Rudy. You're a good brother."

"Generous," he said.

"If you can get Lily home," said Lauren, "that will make up for a very great deal."

Rudy rubbed at the headache curled behind his temple. "I'll do my best. You want me to make her call you when she gets up?"

"Only if she asks. She'll have more than enough of me when she gets back here." He heard the clink of plates and the clack of a cabinet slamming shut. "All the work—years of work—that child will never remember. And if at any point you ease up, if you get tired for a minute, it gives them the sense you've disappointed them. You can blow it all that quickly."

Rudy slipped his phone in his pants pocket and looked in at Lily, still asleep, now curled around her backpack like a sprouting bean. He had left one side of the back door open for air. Now he gently shut it, holding the latch open so it wouldn't wake her. He went to the corner for a coffee. It was only noon.

He sat on the back bumper, turning the white cup in his hands, watching the tan, cold dregs soak their way down from the saliva-frayed edge. Perforated pull-back tab and moist cardboard, not the black sipper. He studied the lid—*why's it got that little pinprick? anyone actually use those buttons for information, or just for a fidget?*—then eventually crushed the cup, doubled-over at the middle, and stuck it under the back wheel.

Driving across the country with a fifteen-year-old girl. Hadn't he read that one before? His *niece*, he would emphasize to the clerk giving him a long stare. Two twin beds. A knock on the door from local cops, barking something about the Mann Act. Buy an extra room. Indecent. All in his mind in the first few seconds. But then: fifteen. His niece. Alone, on the other side of the continent from her family, from his sister, her mother. A chance to redeem— what? He hadn't cost them anything but his presence.

The car shifted, and he saw Lily sit up and pull a chrome water bottle from the pouch of her backpack. On it was a black-and-white sticker, with a woodcut image of a sleeping woman, captioned "I didn't go to work today . . . I don't think I'll go tomorrow."

"I'm starving," she said when she saw him. "Can we get something to eat?"

"Sure," Rudy said. "Diner?"

"My phone says there's fish and chips around the corner."

"Choosy beggar." Rudy laughed. "Your hobo code told you good eats thataway, huh? OK. I'm a little battered and fried myself."

"I forgot," she said. "Something interesting did happen, right at the beginning, at the Silver Spring station. I ordered an almond croissant and the guy behind the counter took a bite out of it while he was ringing me up. Just, like, absentmindedly ate it. I had that to think about for the next three weeks."

She sat sideways in the booth, her legs drawn up and knees together, dripping tartar sauce on the table. "You've been to our house, to where I live," she said. "It's fine. Like, fine even in the old-fashioned sense in which it was a compliment and not condescending. It's a fine place to live, a fine place to grow up. Fuck fine, you know? Fine is a fortress. Fine keeps out anything that's not fine. But nothing is fine. I'm not fine. I don't feel fine. I don't want to be around people who are trying to be good, trying to make everything OK. That's not who I am. That's why I gotta fuck it all up. Typical teenager shit, right? That's what you're thinking? Straight off the script. But that's how this bullshit gets perpetuated." You create a thing called adolescence and a thing called teenagers, she said, more or less; and you say one of the things about teenagers is they always rebel, then they grow out of it, so that if you keep feeling that way after you grow up people get to call you childish and immature. That's why she didn't blame her parents; she didn't think they even noticed when they bought in, when they had to make themselves into enforcers. That was just how the system reproduced itself. The so-called generation gap. Divide and conquer. "That's why I want your life," she said. "You did it right. You just—stepped out, and you don't need anybody. You don't even need us. I want to come with you, but I don't want to need you. I just want to do it like you."

Rudy looked at her, this would-be grisette: slight, even frail, but they shared wide snub knuckles and a frowning brow. And, it seemed, the splinter of ice. Ox stock, he thought. Bovines in our bloodlines. He recognized himself in her complaint and was flattered, but he also resented now having to defend decency, to defend comfort, to defend and nuance a worldview he didn't entirely share himself. Why must children have a blissful childhood? Not a nightmare, of course, but a mediocre one: a sprinkle of idyll, a dash of frustration and privation, limited encounter with evil, to prepare them for life. Seb had once told how he'd been sent to an old-fashioned Catholic school, where the nuns, by way of punishment, would send him to all the funerals in the parish for a month, to contemplate the dead bodies. These happy, cozy kids can sense that their material life doesn't match their emotional life, so they're out looking for discomfort. Everyone wants to be tested. To go orienteering in land that was long ago domesticated. Kids, for their parents, signified—at least in part—an arrival; for the kids, family life was something to escape. The conflict was unavoidable. He understood: it was hard to be happy even with happiness.

But the kids fetishized trouble, too. They were brought up on stories of righteous fights against oppression, the heroism of the persecuted. So how could they get to be heroes, if they couldn't identify how they'd been wronged? No wonder everyone tried so hard to police the boundaries of their affinities. They wanted a piece of the struggle. In a pinch, they could always choose poverty. They? We: hadn't he done that, and for similar reasons. That and some ideas about music. But she, even now, she could always go home. He couldn't. Couldn't he?

Lily, still eating, had slouched almost to recumbent. Rudy noticed himself sitting erect. His shirt was tucked into his pants.

Some men highlight their soft middles with a kind of satisfaction. Young people want, for obscure reasons, to express their disarray, in clothes and posture; in half-proud, reassuring performances of incompetence: around taxes, car maintenance, unmade beds. As a mature man, he wanted to convey control, so he sat up. This, if nothing else, he had achieved. He no longer wished to be distinctive, either. He stripped away identifying markers, got the simplest haircuts, the cheapest jeans, wore plain ball caps from truck stops. His hands relaxed past his belt loops into his pockets.

"There's a song," Rudy said. "It goes, 'I've had all the freedom I can stand.' A lot of days that's how I feel. What do you want to *do* with all that freedom, from everything but yourself?"

Lily wiped her mouth. "Live, right? You live for your art. I don't have that, so I want to make living my art."

"What part of sleeping on a Greyhound is art?"

"Come on. That's just, like, the vector or whatever. The tool. Freedom is freedom from everything, freedom *from* choice. Maybe the bus takes me somewhere I want to go, maybe it doesn't. It's all an experience I'm taking in."

"Weren't you the one complaining this morning that you got on a bunch of buses but nothing happened to you?"

"I was fucking tired. Now I've got a full belly and a nap and I'm telling you what I think."

"But you say you wanted to make living your art. Art is something you push out of yourself, so that you get something from it, but other people do too. You're describing a life as an experience vacuum, sucking it all into yourself and not expelling anything useful. A black hole."

"Yeah, but what does *your* music do for people? Like, I respect what you do, a lot of people respect what you do, but most people don't *like* it. No offense. I mean, like, numerically. They don't *dislike* it, but it doesn't do anything particular for them, or, like, make their life better. So don't get all 'you're selfish' with me. Most of your life is more about *your life* than your art too."

Rudy started to object, but couldn't figure out how she was wrong.

She was sitting up now. "So, OK, I go out into the world, and maybe I meet someone hanging around the center of town, and we go throw stones at some ducks and talk for a couple hours. Did we *do* anything? No. But we'll remember it. We made a connection, like two human beings. That's what I gave them. What I got back. Emotional muses, right? It's not like one inspires the other to go out and create. We both get something from it."

A pretty good model, actually: ten years of kicking around, and still time for a thirty-year working life and a contented retirement. Not bad. Feelings the material of her art. Insubstantial but not commodifiable, not fetishizable. If all you create is feelings, that's an effective way of opting out of the capitalization of the thing. What is physical art, anyway? The size of a disc, the weight of a book—not even that. Flickers of oscillating electricity fluttering in and out of existence. Ideas are so small, words are so small, sound is so small. May as well work in feelings.

"I have to take you home, though," he told her, and she didn't say yes or no. She was the one who'd asked to come with him, and he was heading east, so he guessed she thought they'd work out the details a little later on. He hadn't worked out the details of getting her underage self into the gig tonight, either, so they were even.

LONG, DARK BAR, black-vinyl button-back banquette booths, red chinoiserie above the wainscoting, a lonely rectangle of moldy rug at the back of the stage. Beachball-sized paper lanterns hung from the ceiling. It was hard to tell whether the portholes, portals, in the wall were windows or mirrors. The sign above the door showed a single plane over a setting sun.

He gave her the merch suitcase to wheel in, introduced himself to the bartender—*ah you're Rudy, how goes it, buddy?—it wears as it grows—sorry to hear; sound guy'll be here in thirty, can I get you something in the meantime?—brown ale, and a seltzer and bitters for her*—easy. While he sound checked, Lily folded the T-shirts flat and neat, like a mall-store clerk, and spent some Sharpie time on price tags. She put out a pint glass by way of a tip jar, and taped a sign to it: "Money i$ a fiction and property is theft/So why not give him $ome"—here a cartoon thumb pointed at the stage—"and I ¢🅐n take wh🅐t'$ left."

"Generous of you to take their sins upon yourself," said Rudy. "A goat to the desert."

She grinned, pleased with her domain, and placed her hands palms down on the table possessively, then palms up piously, with a slight, showy curtsey. "I'm a humble martyr."

Rudy had, over the years, gradually increased the number of drinks he'd allow himself (and the phrase "allow himself," if he'd thought about it, was probably telling), not so much out of concern for his performance but because once he had the option of just sleeping in the Timonium it didn't matter if he could drive to a house or hotel. He had a flexible algorithm that began from the premise that driving on two drinks was fine, if they weren't unpredictably alcoholic microbrews; and that he could get away with three. Frankly, sometimes he felt fine to drive at the end of the night anyway, and it wasn't until he woke up with a hangover and a memory gap that he felt lucky.

Out of habit, then, as the night went on, he lost track of both his promise to Lauren about the hotel room and his brown-ale count.

"Break a leg," said Lily, saluting from her stool.

"Two plus a forearm permanently broken," he said.

"Hashtag true professional."

He turned toward the stage, then stopped. "Fuck. I told your mom I'd get us a hotel room, and I forgot, like an asshole."

"So we'll sleep in your car."

Rudy pictured that, and he didn't like the way it would look. "No, I promised . . . " He pulled out his wallet, pawed blurrily at it, then just handed it to her. "Here, you take care of it. Pick a card, any card. For my next trick."

"Sure, I got it." She pulled out her phone.

"You're hired." Rudy looked at her and felt a ping of something like conscience. "Lily."

She looked up. "Yeah?"

"You drive yet?"

"I got my permit."

He nodded with relief. "You're promoted."

21

THEY CHECKED IN, the next night, to a three-story motel in the buzzy mania of Spokane, and parked around the brick back side. The windowless first floor was painted a brighter red; the second and third showed only tiny uncurtained windows. The effect was of a prison wall. As they locked the car, someone tossed a grocery bag swollen with garbage from a top-floor window to the sidewalk. It landed with a crumpling splat. Rudy looked up, but the sash was already slamming sideways. A billboard on stilts perched on the roof. In garish yellow and black, it read, "ARE YOU ASKING FOR IT?" A flourish of cash in a disembodied hand. "Lambert, Lambert and Hayes. Personal Injury Lawyers. SOMEONE SHOULD PAY FOR YOUR PAIN!"

There was a mix-up with the room—just one bed. "Standard double," Lily said. "Double means two beds."

"Fuckin' no," said Rudy, "in hotel lingo double means one, twin means two."

"Well, that doesn't make any fuckin' sense, how'm I supposed to know? Anyway, whatever. It's a big bed."

Rudy didn't answer, just ripped the glossy bedspread off—do that anyway, was his rule—flipped it over on the floor, and curled up on the white side, under the desk.

FAST-FORWARD THROUGH THE mountains and down into Boze-
man; skip the driving montage. "Slow down," said Lily. "I've never
seen this. Look at those trees. That ridge. It's like a toothbrush."

"Colgate snow," Rudy volleyed back.

"Pipe-cleaner pines." She propped her bare feet up on the
inside of the windshield. Foggy toe halos bloomed and dried.
They'd be there for years, Rudy thought, ghosts in frost and steam.

"You know this club tonight?" she asked.

"It's OK. Old gas station. Beer cans and shit on the walls."

She rubbed her knees. "You know what this guy said about
you in Seattle? He said you were a legend. He bought one of everything."

"People always say," he said, "that if you touch one person it's
all worth it. That's just—it's not true. You take in so much empty
flattery, so much blank indifference, spend so much time away
from anyone whose opinions you can trust. Eventually it's impossible to take a compliment. It's like, oh you love me now, you
won't later; or you're just saying that, or you want something from
me, or you feel bad and you think this'll make it better. You get
to believe that only dilettantes and the naive enthuse. The circus
has no use for bows, they hustle you on, hustle you off, wean you
off applause. That's long-haul professional. Those big ideas about
transcendence, about what music can mean, the punk utopia—I
love it, God, I love it; I admire it, but I can't believe it. That's
the damage of all this: not that my body's a wreck, or I drink too
much, or whatever. It's that I don't believe anyone. I don't even—I
wouldn't recognize sincerity. I don't have that notch on my
receptor, it's worn off."

"Why don't you do something else if you hate it so much?
Write a novel. Wash dishes."

"Novels you gotta be specific about what happens. Songs you can
just sketch around the edges. I can't work three years on anything.

A song you can finish in an afternoon. Not always, but you can reasonably expect it to happen from time to time. Anyway, inertia is a powerful thing. How would I recognize the day I'm gonna get up and say, I'm done, I'll drown my book?"

Lily closed her eyes. She slid lower in the chair and laid her cheek on the seatbelt strap. He would be talking to himself soon. "Think about the thing you love the most," he said, "and imagine hating it. Imagine how you could come to hate it, and how you would feel about hating it. Would you hate the feeling as much as the thing? No—you'd hate the feeling more. You'd find a comfort in turning that hate away from yourself, into a smug superiority over people who still love that thing. Like you know better now. Pretend you'd grown when you'd just—dried up."

The downrushing snow flung itself from the sky. He looked at Lily, her mouth hanging open, gently breathing. Thought of his first car. The stereo had been stolen and never replaced. He kept a boom box in the passenger seat, a battery hog, so many squat, heavy Ds. He kept a dozen loose in the glove compartment. He strapped it back with the seatbelt so it wouldn't jostle and dive when he swerved. Still couldn't play CDs in it, though—too unsteady not to skip. More than once, he ran out of live batteries, and when the tapes garbled out, it was just him and the silent box riding shotgun. That was when he'd started singing and making up words. Keeping himself company on long motley drives. Nice to have, company.

Lily coughed, shifted, reached down and reclined her seat, all without really waking.

"NOPE," SAID THE bearded bartender. "Come on, man, that girl's not twenty-one. You know the fuckin' rules. She can't come in."

"It's my niece," Rudy implored. "I'm driving her home."

The man looked at him hard and long. "I don't know what the

fuck you're up to. But I never saw any dads bringing their daugh-
ters on tour. Definitely no nieces. You take that shit somewhere
else. You can play, but she's gotta stay outside."

Lily read her anarchist romances supine on the car's mattress,
with the curtains drawn and the engine running for heat, swirling
exhaust and a comforting rumble. Local openers the Myoclonic
Jerks—who were, jerks that is—played for a handful of what
looked like coworkers still in their ties. Obligation rock. Rudy did
his bit in front of the quilt of stamped-tin gas ads. A shaggy-haired
drunk harassed a pair of off-duty pilots: "You guys see any UFOs?
Can't talk about it, right?" As they tried to ignore him, he pulled
up one side of his shirt, exposing a torso less muscular than gaunt,
on which a deep red sunburn blurred a muddle of tattoos. "Check
it out—I got a fuckin' leaky Twinkie right here, a couple candy
corn over here. How many snack tats you got?" He approved his
own monologue—"yeahhh"—and tore off a ripped-fabric fart.

Lily was shivering in the morning. Winter was passing, but
fitfully and intransigently, and she had left home without a single
pair of pants, just black tights. "We got three days to get to Iowa
City," Rudy said. "Let's go down to the hot springs, soak some of
the chill out."

They stopped at a laundromat in Billings, stripped off as much
clothing as they could legally spare into an ostrich-neck cart, then
stuffed it into the industrial stainless steel washers. A gray-haired
woman in shapeless pants walked over and, without meeting their
eyes, offered some advice: "You saw how I poured some Coke in
there? It's just as good as bleach and gets that grease out." They
thanked her and she shuffled away, shoes slipping and crunching
on spilled powdered detergent.

They left the double-wide suburbs, passed slowly through
the Cody death cult. "I thought there was supposed to be, like, no

speed limit out here," said Lily. "Everybody's doing seventy on the dot."

"Yeah," Rudy said, "once they brought it back in Montana, I guess everybody snapped to. In Wyoming they must just be constitutionally law-abiding. Or else, how much faster are you really gonna go?" He accelerated past a wide-bellied pickup tugging a blocky camper. The wire-brush hills broke out in a ruddy rash, oxidized iron in sandstone. For a landscape that was a whole lot of nothing, there sure were a lot of different varietals of nothing. Nothing can change.

"No skateboarding on the highway," read the sign on the road that dipped into Thermopolis. A redundant banner—"Open Sundays"—stretched across the side of a church. An antique store boasted, "More odds than ends." White stones across the face of a butte identified the "World's Largest Mineral Hot Springs," arrow arrow. "ERNIE DO YOU WANT SOME ICE CREAM," joked a marquee. "SURE BERT." The addendum placard announcing "Welcome Sturgis Bikers" was like a Christmas tree in April, either a forgotten remnant or an eager gun-jumper.

Rudy was sorry to miss them. He liked bike rallies: fleshy, sunbaked grandparents in genial goatees and leather. Organized processions of rebel posturing and theoretical mayhem. More than one friend of his had seen their first bare breasts at the Tomahawk ride.

A skateboarder paused at a stop sign on Broadway—no, Broadway Street. A pickup pulled up behind him and politely nudged him forward. If the people here weren't dressed like ranchers—plaid button-down shirts tucked into dark denim, white mustaches under ball cap brims, stiff-walking with rodeo injuries—they'd almost pass for old hippies. The seductions of the counterculture had reached as far as craft beer, here, before breaking on the blunt levees of habit.

They checked into a hotel on the hot spring grounds. Its walls were flaky with safari photos and animal heads, stuffed bears and mounted horns, fading photos of lions pulling down zebras or driven off by bristling porcupine. A montage of red nature that doubled, Rudy assumed, as a claustrophobic expression of a political philosophy. The shirtless, broad torso of the owner grinned out from every direction, flanked by Black guides, kneeling over limp bloody corpses. Identify all the animals in the barroom, read the menu, and our bartender will buy you a drink.

"Fucking rednecks," said Lily. "What are they trying to prove. I don't know why you like playing these shithole towns."

Rudy felt a prickle of defensive annoyance. "I've had some of the best times of my life in shitholes."

"No culture. How they gonna understand what you do. Play Portland and San Francisco."

"First of all, it's not like I have a lot of choices. Take shows where they'll have me. Anyway, don't be condescending. You don't know these people. They know how to leave a guy alone. In the cities, I always feel like I'm being sized up and judged and ranked on a pecking order out to three decimal places."

Lily flipped the laminated drink menu back and forth. "Thought everyone knew your business in a small town."

"Yeah, but they don't bother themselves with it. Gotta have boundaries when everyone knows each other. Pretend not to see what you can see. Etiquette over intimacy. You nod at each other, give a little wave, leave it at that. Less loneliness, more solitude."

Lily slid a flyer across the table: Acoustic jam session, it advertised, at the south side Exxon, first Friday of every month. With your host Harry Bumpers of Sheridan, Wyoming. "Here you go, then," she said. "Get to know your neighbors."

"Only thing worse than talking to strangers," Rudy said, "is playing music with them. Blues licks instead of folk wisdom about the weather, it's all just filling up space so you don't have to come up with something original to say."

"Who's being judgmental now."

They soaked in the spring among a silent congregation of senior citizens. The steaming sulfurous water was, historically, receding, rationed now between the free public bath and the two loud private water parks. The white chalky terraces baked around stagnant pools and trickling spills.

They drove out of town in the morning. The leaves were beginning to bud, and flashed first silver, then lime. The broken straw fields would soon be shocking swaths of green circumscribed by pissing irrigation pivots. The mountains on the horizon presented in translucent layers: first drab umber, then bruise blue, lavender, glaucous. They passed into the corroded, black-stained limestone of the Bighorns, miles of castellated cliff faces in a skim milk haze.

They pulled over at a lakeside boat ramp and decided to walk the shore. Grasshoppers clacked like rattlesnakes and scattered before their steps, leaping from dun bug to yellow fly in the eerie purple of high-altitude low scrub. Two parents in a canoe sang tunelessly to a squalling baby, then the wind changed and there was no telling if it had worked. Mating blue dashers scattered white and orange butterflies over the cornflower. An elderly couple in red-white-and-blue folding chairs and camouflage hats set new bait and pulled fresh cans from a cooler. A log lay like a pipeline, its heartwood rotted out.

Then back down into the plains, eastbound through Wyoming toward South Dakota, the clefts and furrows and plateaus like the immense shallow low-tide beach of a subsided inland sea. A motorboat slid down into a dry, furry gully. The rare lakes here were contingent—lucky puddles. The Basque quatrefoil on bumpers and lawn-parked sheep wagons. A truck pulled over to bolster the barn, an American flag painted on its side, lashed to its trailer. Mobile homes in a junkyard or shantytown just off the exit ramp squatted and shed. A steady march of green Sinclair dinosaurs. A shark with bared teeth painted on the blade of a county snowplow. Red gravel ranch roads disappeared toward the monumental Soviet mundanity of a coal extraction and processing facility, toward long balloon stacks of propane bobtails, toward a barn sheathed in blinding sheet metal, toward slow, corrugated lives.

In no hurry, Lily and Rudy turned northeast off the highway toward Devil's Tower. Rudy found the emergence of a ponderosa forest viscerally comforting—visible green life, vertically asserting itself, and shelter. The baby pines clustered, foot-tall ambitious twigs with a bustle of needles at their tip. Two shirtless young men sat atop a laundromat billboard. A helmeted boy bounced a dirt bike through the shortgrass. A calvary of incinerated tree trunks silhouetted along the spine of a ridge. Then, from the horizon, the vast upwelling column, all but the core eroded, like the hub of the continent itself, migratory birds circling, the gravitational whirl that attracts, the spin that scatters. With its vertical grooves, it could be a monument to an extinct technology from the prehistory of recorded sound, an evolutionary dead end, an obsolete cylinder, a song trapped forever for want of a playback engine.

At the base of the tower a clutch of candy-colored motorcycles clustered around a tourist-trap trading post—FUDGE ICE CREAM BEER T-SHIRTS BUFFALO HIDES SARSAPARILLA ATM WIFI HOTSPOT—guarded by carved bear greeters hewn chainsaw-rough. Boy Scouts in matching shirts and mismatched basketball shorts weaved around bikers wearing their libertarian patriotic camp of flames and eagles. Vintage convertibles, painted inauthentically bright, lounged with hoods yawning to show off their engines to the restrained examination of stiff-backed, butt-out cowboys.

Up into alpine fields that, but for the buttes, would pass for a ragged Scottish golf course. A bright yellow plane on a pole. The acute, south-facing isosceles houses of high-snow areas. The blue shadows of the Black Hills. "South Dakota: Great Places Great Faces," read the sign, and Lily made them stop. Rudy had been through forty-nine states, but somehow never to South Dakota—the drive was always Minneapolis to Seattle through Fargo. He posed by the billboard of the presidents, and flashed an open palm and a closed fist—five and zero—while she thumbed a picture into her phone.

They got a cabin in the pines outside Lead—rhymes with "need," not "bed"—the precarious twin to cocksure Deadwood's historical kitsch and tawdry casinos; both towns convened beneath clear-cut hilltops littered with matchstick trunks. A white limousine swung into the Dakotamart lot and parked lengthwise across four spots. No one came out. Someone had written "ECLIPSED" in careful soap capitals across the top of their windshield, an artifact from the previous year's solar event.

Lead's main street ("72 Hour Parking"—that should be plenty, Lily joked) was for rent or for sale, people trying to unload their hotels, storefronts (a handwritten sign in one urged "Vote Chickens"—and why not, Rudy said), vacation getaways. Houses up into the hills were painted bright encouraging purples, yellows, greens, and maroons. A hippie store—"Aspire"—faced off against Southern Arms Guns & Ammo, and, Lily figured, was responsible for the half-finished mural languishing above the abandoned scaffolding in the adjacent vacant lot. The Gold Brick Launderette advertised "Hair Dryers/Soft Water."

A man in a lawn chair waved—more "I'm watching you" than "hello, stranger"—from beside a sign proclaiming "Yard of the Week."

A man at a crosswalk—"Party like it's 1776," read his shirt, in red white and blue letters—pointed up an alley and said, "A big deer just ran across the street."

"Big buck," said the woman with him. "Huge rack."

Fraternal and sororal organizations beat time down the street—the Odd Fellows, Masons, Rebekah Lodge, American Legion, Veterans of Foreign Wars—leading to a chain-link fence topped with three strands of barbed wire.

Behind it was a colossal pit ringed with terraces, a faintly heart-shaped bowl a thousand feet deep and wide, and shafts thousands of feet beneath that, the negative image of the devoured mountain. The Homestake Mine—there's enough gold here to make a stake, the founders thought, to scrape it all out and then go home. Home, that is, somewhere else. They were right, just not for themselves. It was too big to simply take and leave. Too big for the hundred years of workers who made this their home, too. When the mining company did pack up and go— to wherever a corporation calls home—they left this open cut. It wasn't really their home, and you're only responsible for cleaning your own home. Soon, the Open Cut, this unbandaged, dried-out wound, began to undermine the real homes of Lead. They had failed to reinforce the foundations. They took, and didn't replace. The footings cracked, the bedrock crumbled: subsidence was the term of art, like a subsided sea, like a subsistence living. The heart of the town had to be moved. Everything valuable had been taken from the core, and the whole thing just started to collapse.

22

TOO SLOW, TOO REPETITIVE, skip ahead. Get to the next show, get to Iowa City: when was the last time anyone was eager to get to Iowa City? But fine, fine, skirt the Black Hills to the off-season purgatory of Sturgis; then Rapid City, Wall Drug, the Badlands and reservations. Did they turn south at Sioux Falls, pick up the Missouri at Sioux City and thence to Council Bluffs and Omaha, straight across the corn fields through Des Moines? Or did they continue east, slicing across southern Minnesota, take 35 south and cut across the northeast quadrant on state routes? Did it take two days or three? They listened to Artie Shaw, the clarinetist who walked away. They watched a movie with Jeff Bridges: I like him, Rudy said. They stopped for breakfast. Lily spilled syrup on the table and mopped it up with a folded pancake.

Iowa City felt like a return to a predictable, orderly world: the wide avenues of a midwestern university town, the angled parking, the two- or three-story brick buildings, the quick student food. Back-alley parking, a picket gate, pool table, jukebox, and booths downstairs; a wide open room with a raised stage upstairs. Load the gear up a metal staircase, over the graffitied beer garden.

Lily examined the framed calendar in the front window. "Holy shit," she said. "You're playing with The Ghost of Tom Choad tonight!"

"Yeah," said Rudy. "Little guy. Gross beard. Bandana around his neck. I was on a bill with him in Asheville a while ago."

"Dude. I love him. He's an inspiration. He's the real deal. Like, hopping trains and hitchhiking with his dogs to tour. Living outside of capitalism. I saw a video of him standing on top of a cop car singing 'Hobo With a Squirtgun.' They, like, dragged him off, and he kept playing until one of the cops put a boot through his guitar. Awesome."

Lily skipped up the stairs, humming to herself. She spent a little extra time decorating the white folding table and straightening the merch. The heavy door beside the stage clanged open, and a squall of sunlight burst into the stale showroom.

"Hey, you fuckin' scumbags, cool it," said a raw, high-pitched voice. A pair of pit bulls scrabbled across the hardwood, dragging a ferrety young man in black cargo pants and a black tank top with white block letters that read "Drunk, Broke and Beautiful." He wore an overstuffed army backpack and a black cycling cap with a popped brim. A distressed, backless banjo—a six-string—covered with stickers hung on a frayed rope over one shoulder.

"Hey, hey," said the sound man, hurrying over. "Those dogs gotta stay outside."

"Aw, come on, man. They've been out in the sun busking with me all afternoon, let 'em cool off. Yeah, good dogs," he said to them, mussing the fur on their necks. "This is Chicken, and this asshole is Polisher, first name Bone."

"It's just health code. You know the deal."

He pulled off his cap and wiped a strand of hair forward over his forehead. "Alright, fuck, at least gimme a bowl of water for 'em." He looked over at Lily. "Hey lady, you the merch slinger tonight? I'm Tom."

Lily swung her leather fanny pack around her right hip. "I

know, I saw you at Daedal House in Arlington."

"Oh shit, is that the one where everyone ended up on the roof? That was fuckin' off the chain. Like cats, right, easier to get up than get down!" He let out a phlegmy cackle. "Least we had the forties for company. Here, lemme bring my boys here outside and I'll come set my shit up." He accepted a stainless-steel mixing bowl full of water from the soundman and yanked the dogs back through the door. He returned a few minutes later, threw his backpack under the table, and leaned his banjo against the wall. It slipped sideways and landed on the floor with a discordant chime.

Tom cursed, and Lily rushed to help him pick it up. "Ah, fuck it," he said. "It was only ten bucks at a pawnshop anyway." He laughed. "Frugal oogle, that's this guy!"

Lily smiled back and introduced herself, held out her hand. He took and kissed it with a flourish. "So you're here with Rudy P?"

Lily glanced at Rudy. "Yeah, you know, I've been traveling for a while, met up with him in Seattle and he's giving me a ride. Don't know where I'm headed exactly, but—"

Rudy stepped forward. "Hey Tom. Lily's my niece, I'm taking her home."

Lily reddened and looked away.

Tom grinned at Rudy. He had a pair of parenthetical dimples and a rusty tan. He was missing an upper incisor. Still, he had a mongrel charm. "Yeah, man! Asheville, right? Well alright. I think we're all gonna have a real good time tonight. So, Miss Lily, I've got some stuff to put out. May I have the pleasure of sharing this table with you?" He reached into his backpack and began pulling out his merchandise: white-on-black shirts, records, buttons, enamel pins, fraying patches of various sizes.

"Impressive," said Rudy, honestly. "You got the magic bottomless backpack."

Tom unfolded a rough square of ripped cardboard that read "CASH IS KING" in Sharpied capitals. "Well, I gotta carry a lot around. Internet orders, ya know? It's not like my dirty-ass room-mates are gonna keep up on the Etsy while I'm traveling. Fuckin' deadbeats." He looked at his stock with satisfaction. "Rude, you gotten drink tickets from this dump yet?"

Rudy produced three yellow stubs from his back pocket. Tom gave them a connoisseur's brisk assessment, then unbuckled another pocket in his bag. He withdrew a crumpled white grocery bag and opened it. Inside were a pile of tight rolls of paper tickets in a prism of colors. He selected a saffron coil that more or less matched Rudy's, ripped off a couple dozen, and folded them into a neat wad that he shoved into a thigh pocket. He rolled up the grocery bag and returned it to its place. "Best investment I make before tour," he said, tapping his temple. "Drinks on me tonight."

TOM AMBLED UP the stage stairs from the floor, holding, nearly dragging, his banjo by the neck. He held a triple pour in a small plastic cup. He lay the instrument on the stage and patted himself down, finally locating a pick in a back pocket. He stuck the pick in the gap in his teeth, slung the banjo over his neck, and and croaked into the mic: "Hey you dirtbags, what's the difference between a rich alcoholic and a poor drunk?" He coughed. "Nothing. One's an eccentric and the other's in the street. I know which one I'd rather be. This one's called 'Whiskey, You're an Angel!'"

He strummed a rapid-fire backbeat and a dozen or so khaki crusties materialized from the wall shadows and clustered at the foot of the stage, fists in the air, yelling along tunelessly and shoving each other. Rudy saw Lily stash a tumbler of her own under the table and race across the vacant floor to join them as they morphed into a hopeful sketch of a circle pit. Their dreamland, Rudy thought, operated under the fantasy that they could imagine the world as they wanted it to be—imagine the acoustic guitar was a band, imagine their covey was a sold-out show, imagine they were real derelicts, imagine a real derelict wouldn't be hungry and tired, imagine this would still look good on them in ten or fifteen years, imagine the revolution was coming, imagine that songs would have any part in bringing it on. Or maybe just imagine that the revolution was unnecessary, that songs could keep the world at bay.

The crusties received Rudy politely. He liked that about punks—they would tell you if they thought you were terrible, but they'd give you a chance. Sometimes they'd tell you explicitly that they were giving you a chance. Plus, they were romantics by nature. They sat cross-legged in a semicircle on the floor and looked up at him. One couple lay down, hands behind their head, and closed their eyes. A woman leaned on her backpack. The set drifted past. Rudy thought he'd try out a new one on them.

> *I have known the blade, the blossom, and the fruit; and now*
> *   I know their withering*
> *There are mountain hours that take all day to climb*
> *And downhill days you descend singing*
> *One eye on the crowd and one on the moon*
> *Your father was the rough sea, and you are the schooner*
>
> *New river, spring for me*
> *Carry me down to the reeling sea*
> *Spill your way across the open country*
> *A bronze-bound vessel with a bone in her teeth*

Attentive applause, and at least one appreciative whoop. Rudy peered toward the merch table: some part of him, like an over-eager dad, wanted to see Lily seeing that people she considered part of her world respected him. He was no longer young, he was no longer representative of a scene—not since the Expats—and his lyrics couldn't be howled by a group, used as a rallying cry, stickered on a bike, or excerpted as an online handle, but they could be understood.

This was one of those stages, though, with a spotlight right in his face. Anything beyond a few feet from the front of the stage melted into a mute penumbra. Rudy didn't like that. He wanted to be able to track reactions line by line, see what hit. He wanted to know if people were losing interest and leaving, or drifting his way. Even in a case like this, where there were a dozen people in a room that could hold four hundred—well, that was useful information too. At least he could acknowledge it, let everyone know they could relax.

He knelt and downed his glass in one gulp. This got a round of half-sincere, half-ironic cheers. "Thank you for your kind attention," he said. "You seem like nice people, and I appreciate it. Let me know if there's anything I can do for you before I let you go back to your busy lives."

A young man with a curved piece of bone through his septum raised himself onto an elbow. "You got anything a little cheerier?"

"Cheerier?" said Rudy.

"Yeah, you know, this mopey white-dude trip is a bummer. Leave us feeling good, man!"

Rudy was in a good enough mood that this didn't bother him. "You know what they say, write what you know." He stepped back and spread his arms, as if to say, look at me, what am I supposed to do?

That got a few chuckles.

"Alright, man, alright," said septum bone. "You seem like a guy who's been around. Send us out with something that we can, you know, use."

Rudy stepped back into the mic and grinned, held a hand to his brow and looked again into the depopulated hall. Lily's chair was empty. Shame she'd miss his paternal moment. "Yeah. Here's a good one: you can say whatever you want as long as you don't care about having people around."

Laughs and claps from the floor.

"Then you'll have plenty of time to work out how you got to be such an asshole that that was the one thing you wanted."

A round of applause and cheers.

"Thanks everybody!" Rudy waved with real warmth. "I had a great time with you tonight. Please enjoy the rest of your evening."

The bar music swelled to fill the room, and Rudy squatted to unplug and coil. The lights went up. Three of the crusties were spending a few courteous minutes fondling his merchandise. Probably they wouldn't buy, but you never knew.

They offered compliments and questions, but he brushed them off. No, he couldn't sell them Tom patches either, sorry. Thanks, appreciate it, see you next time, good luck, et cetera. The bartender said maybe he'd seen Lily going out on the back patio, hey, good show. Thanks, appreciate it, et cetera. Lemme have another one of these, drink ticket plus two bucks. He drank that, and thought at least he'd start loading out, slung his cable and pedal bag over a shoulder and picked up his guitar. Through the door onto the metal landing, down the stairs into the beer garden. A purr of conversation from some people at the wooden picnic tables, locals who'd been in the downstairs bar that night. Tom's dogs asleep by their bowl. He unslid the bolt-latch and opened the gate to the alley where he'd left the car. He set the guitar on the pavement, dug for his keys, exhaled through his nose at the scent of stagnant dumpster juice.

The key crackled into the back door lock and Rudy chunked it open. There was a scramble of clothes and blankets on the mattress, and two pairs of eyes reflected fixed in the new light like raccoons surprised by the flash of a curious camera. Tom's bare sunken chest and soft potbelly were spotted, cheetah-like, with blurring tattoos. Lily yanked her shirt down over her blanched torso.

Rudy's first reaction was no reaction. Tom's reaction—"Oh hey, sorry man"—confused him further. Why sorry? Sorry like I'm a father defending her honor, or sorry like we're tour mates and he's borrowed my bed? If he'd caught Lily's actual dad in a similar situation—which he had—it would have been grounds for a high five later, which it had been. Or sorry just because that's what you say when you don't know how someone's going to react?

Lily, meanwhile, was looking from side to side, and swaying a little. Finally she unlatched the sliding side door and stumbled out, buttoning the waistband of her pants. "I gotta pee," she mumbled.

Rudy followed her up the stairs, back into the showroom. The house music had been turned off, and their steps echoed in the vacant hall. Lily ran across the floor, knocking over three gray plastic trash cans that had been emptied of their bags. She pivoted around the wall that divided the bathroom entrances and swung through the men's room door.

She was standing close against a urinal, pants and underwear around her knees, pissing a loose stream onto the half-melted ice and cigarette butts. Her eyes were closed and her mouth hung open. He quickly turned his back to her.

"We had a deal," he said. "Who's going to drive us?"

Lily didn't look at him, but exhaled with a burst of amazed disdain. "That's what you're mad about here? Who's taking care of who?" She joggled her bare ass back and forth to shake off last drops, and squatted to pull up her pants. "I thought you were rescuing me, the family man, cool dad. And you want to know who's gonna drive you home 'cause you're drunk after the big show?"

He was silent, and she turned to look at him, wiping her hands on her thighs. "I'm not going back to Maryland. You know that, right? No fucking way. You better fucking watch out for me, if you think you're driving me back to my parents' house. I'll be out like a fucking ninja. Maybe I'll roll with Tom for a while, see what that's like. At least he knows how to have a good time. And if that doesn't last, I'll find someone else. No one's gonna let me starve. I'm too little and nice and pretty and I've got a voice like a little kid, and there's always someone who wants to take care of me."

She pushed past him and out the door, triggering the hand dryer's jet-engine blast as she went.

Fucking judge *me*, he thought. Let her go. Fucking not *my* kid. Let her get robbed, raped, go hungry, have some *experiences* that she can have some *feelings* about.

Not mine, he thought—but stubborn like me. Rude, like me.

Lauren didn't believe he could take care of himself, let alone Lily. If Lily got away from him, Lauren wouldn't even be disappointed in him. You have to expect something to be disappointed.

When he got to the alley, the back door of the car was hanging open. The dogs were gone and so, presumably, was Tom. A small pile of pink vomit trailed around a rear wheel into the gutter. Rudy shut the door, looked down the street—right, then left— picked one and jogged toward the streetlight. He circled the block, then the next, before he saw the small dark catlike figure on a municipal bus bench.

Lily was curled up around her backpack, her hoodie zipped to her neck and the string pulled tight around her face. Rudy picked her up and she put her head limply on his shoulder. "Fucking assholes, all of you," she murmured. He carried her back to the car, laid her on the mattress, and covered her with the rough blanket. He closed the back doors with as soft a click as he could manage and walked around to the passenger seat. He sat, closed and locked the doors, and reclined the seat as far as it would go. He rolled his head back and forth, tried one shoulder, then the other. He pulled the seatbelt across himself and latched it. He threaded the chest strap behind his neck and let his head fall back and bounce on it like a hammock. A little support, a little restraint.

23

HE WOKE UP before she did, slid over and drove them to a motel. Super 7, so, like a discount. They didn't have anywhere to be now and needed to get clean. He parked, checked in, and walked over to the Kum & Go for a coffee. He forgot to get creamer and burned his tongue. He spit, shook his head, flicked open his phone, and called Lauren.

She picked up on the second ring and didn't say hello. "How is she?"

"I think," said Rudy, "she should stay with me for a while."

There was a stunned silence. "Are you fucking out of your mind?" Lauren asked.

"I think you won't be able to keep her there."

"I'm going to fucking well try."

"Listen. She's not happy there. For whatever reason, I don't know why. But I do know about being unhappy and not knowing why and trying to run away from it, and that doesn't go away. She's got the same thing I've got. Parenthetically, she's got your taste for strays, too. She thinks she's had it too easy, I guess."

"Too easy!" said Lauren. "Any human alive should be so lucky to have it too easy. Why wouldn't I want my children to be happy? Why should they have to worry about how their happiness came to be? They can be protected from their privilege, as they like to say, as far as I'm concerned. Let it come as an unpleasant surprise, if it must come. What am I supposed to do, expose them to all the world's misery in one foul dump of shit? Or let it drip out, one evil a day? They've got their whole lives to figure out that the world can be a nightmare. Why can't they just let their childhoods be happy."

Rudy waited to see if she was done. "She's already been out of school," he said. "It's not like she's going to slide back into her semester at this point. Let her ride around with me. Maybe it'll be like a vaccine, you know? Drunks and not sleeping, it gets old. Put her off it, so she won't do it later when it counts for more. At least she'll figure out how to do it right, not spanging with some scum-bags in Asheville, turning up toothless in Eugene. I'll show her the country and maybe some carpentry. Spring and summer, and then she can go back to school."

Rudy heard only tired breathing on the line. "Lauren," he said. "Let me help."

"You want to help," she said, "you can go to Madison. Maybe I'd have a better relationship with my daughter if I wasn't also trying to keep our father alive."

An intransigence he couldn't explain or ignore welled up in Rudy. "I'm offering the thing I have to offer."

"Why," said Lauren, "are you so resistant to the idea of helping our parents? It's not the absolute least you could do, but it's close."

"I just—" It was a good question, and he didn't have a good answer. "She can actually use the things I can give her. She needs them—me. I haven't felt that in a long time."

"You want the gratification of being a parent," said Lauren, "before you've fulfilled your responsibilities as a child. You haven't earned it yet."

"I thought the point of being a child was not having responsibilities."

"You would," she said. "I can't talk to you about this now. Talk to Jules."

There was a long period of rustling and muffled voices before Jules came on the line. Rudy paced up and down the grass median between the motel and gas station parking lots, keeping an eye on the still-closed back door of his car. Jules's voice was rougher and deeper, but some of his breezy fecklessness remained. "Hey, Rudy," he said. "I hear you're taking our daughter."

"Technically, she came to me."

"Hang on, I'm going outside." The banging of a screen door. "Don't tell Lauren I said this, but I actually think it's not a bad idea."

"You don't?"

"I mean, look, it's not ideal, obviously, but you can only piss with the cock you've got, right? Between you and me, Lauren and I have been having problems for a while, and I bet Lily could use some fresh air. We'd been trying for so long that by the time the boy finally came I think we'd forgotten why it was important to us. And then, the next thing you know, you've got a four-year-old lying lengthwise across your pillows and tap-dancing on your temples every night. Poor kid. He'll be bald like me. His hair's on loan. Anyway, it's hard to spend quality time together. If Lily goes with you, at least it'll be all hands on deck with the boy. Have nights and naptimes to ourselves."

Jules coughed. "I know I'm rambling. It's just, like, I never get to talk about this stuff with anybody. I don't really want to bring it up with guys from the old days, remind us both how much has changed. Sometimes I still think of that as the real me, and this is just, like, me desperately trying to stay in character."

"It's OK." Rudy saw the back doors of the car shudder and crack open like an egg.

"You know, we even talked about opening up our marriage. But it sounded exhausting, or doubly humiliating. Like, you're free to sleep with other people because your wife's not interested anymore. Monogamy is the worst form of relationship, except for all the others." He paused. "Sorry, I know that's your sister."

"None taken." And Rudy did feel some sympathy for Jules. He could imagine the train of not-quite-deliberate choices Jules had made; that he'd been struck once by the urge for Lauren, and because at that time Jules liked to try to cross all those urges off a list, one thing had led to another, and look how inexorably his life had changed.

Lily stuck her head out, blinking, trying to figure out where she was.

"How's work?"

Jules sighed. "You run the risk, hiring people for advertising, that they hate the job, hate themselves for taking the job, and hate anyone who thinks they're good at the job, so much that they can't do the job. Anyway"—he spruced up his tone—"you know who I saw online the other day? Remember Max? Used to be in Ryan's band?"

"Oh yeah. Is he not still teching for him?"

"Nah, that's not a career. He tapped out and bought a bread route in, like, Vidalia, somewhere in the sticks. Says it's OK but the hours are for shit. Three a.m. wakeups."

"Midlife crisis comes early for crew."

"Yeah, you can just about push into your thirties before the reckoning. Ryan got sober, and the guys got sick of having to keep a dark rider in the trailer. I do keep up with some of the dudes. Pashlo is big in Germany. They love that Americana act. Hear from Jimmy Locust from time to time."

"Oh yeah? He still run with Top Shelf?"

"Shit." Jules laughed. "I open a text from him, I don't know if it's gonna be a racial slur or some chick's vag, or both."

"Can't make a swamp rat use a litterbox."

"Well, he ain't housebroken, that's for sure."

"You hear from Ryan ever?"

"It's not like he was an easy guy to get a hold of, after a while. But no, not since whatever happened between you guys." He cleared his throat and vehemently spit. "But seriously, though. Lily coming with you. I think it'll be good for you, too. Children are a hedge against the darkness. But you try and keep the darkness away from her, too. As best you can."

LILY WAS SITTING knees-up on the bumper, the back doors open wide. "I can't believe you're still using that phone," she said. "It's literally older than I am."

"I like to think that obsolescence doesn't come on a schedule," said Rudy. "It's not the most unreasonable thing about me."

"Eventually the networks won't connect with it."

"So when that happens, I'll get the oldest possible shit and run it into the ground too," said Rudy. "Time comes for us all." He sat next to her.

She buried her chin in her knees. "Sorry about last night."

"I would not," he said, "consider myself in a position to accept an apology, given my generally transparent house."

"Still."

"I talked to your parents just now."

Lily looked at him with distress. "I don't—"

"Don't worry. I suggested that you might stay out with me through the summer. If you don't want to go all gypsies, tramps, and thieves instead."

She didn't smile, but the corners of her mouth tightened a little.

"You have to call your mother, though. She needs some reassuring and convincing."

Her mouth loosened and sank. "Ugh. I'm not ready for that yet. I gotta use the bathroom. Do you have keys yet?"

Rudy handed her a paper packet with a plastic card. "212, like Manhattan. It's just like the Plaza in there."

She took it. "You got any razors?"

He dug around next to the mattress and came up with a ripped-open plastic packet that held a few less than its original dozen yellow disposable razors. He pulled one out and handed it to her. "Why?"

"Clean myself up. Fresh start."

She emerged a half hour later with a shaved head, the skin even paler than the rest of her but for three raw red wounds. She clutched a wad of single-ply toilet paper in her hand. A slim thread of blood snaked behind her left ear.

"Jesus," Rudy said. "There's a better way to do that."

"I got it as short as I could with scissors first."

"Next time tell me, I've got clippers. Hacking away with that piece of shit, no wonder you scalped yourself. Like scraping the hairs out of an artichoke with a spoon."

She wiped behind her ear. "Let me have your phone."

This time she disappeared for almost an hour. When she returned, some of the toilet paper was stuck to two of the gashes, soaked through. The third was beginning to scab. She wiped her red eyes and nose roughly with the rest of the paper and handed Rudy the phone, still open. "Here."

He took it. "Hello?"

"Let me be clear," said Lauren, sounding tired. "I stand in judgment of you both. I'm not just being Mama No-Fun. I think this life is bad for you."

Rudy was silent.

"She promised to call me every morning. I need you to hold her to that."

"OK."

"Rudy. Please take care of her. I guess I'd rather have you two together keeping each other safe and alive than alone and in trouble."

part VI

24

THE FULL MOON was a wrecking ball, a skein of geese its chain. Lily left the bar after a loud night, her ears hissing and pulsing, peoples' voices flattened like Tunguska pines. She packed the merch—the suitcase of records, the failing cardboard box with leaves cross-folded over the shirts—into the back of the van, while her uncle made friendly noises and accepted a free drink or two. Lily herself had quit drinking: she didn't like drunks, she'd decided. They were too unpredictable, loud then sullen, solicitous then mean. They made you mother them. They were sex pests.

What life pressed on her didn't show, but settled in her. To her surprise, she found satisfaction in being the responsible one in her world. One slips into open slots, and there was a vacancy. What did it mean for her to be good? So far, a year and a half in, it meant being good at things, little things, folding the shirts and facing the bills, keeping the receipts organized in the glove box, collecting the hundred or two from whatever gargoyle with gray dreadlocks was the club contact. Being good was outlined and trailed by failure—she could see that any night. It was a full-time job being good, and not everyone likes to go to work every day.

After the first summer on the road, Rudy took Lily to the farm. She helped with the harvest, hung some sheetrock, stacked breeze blocks, got her age waiver and passed the GED. Started thinking about applying somewhere. She had friends in Gainesville. No rush, though.

THE CLUB IN EL PASO had paintings of, Lily guessed, rock stars on plywood on the walls. Their show was up in the third-floor lounge; there was a bigger act sound checking downstairs, which seemed like it would interfere with their set. She set up the merch table and opened her laptop to kill time, maybe scope out something cool to do in Austin or Atlanta later that week. She searched "rudy pauver atlanta" for the venue address, and the local free rag's "Picks of the Week" or whatever came up, and guess who was playing the theater down the street, four nights while they'd be there—Ryan Orland! Hey Rudy, she said, and told him, and he was weird about it, like she expected, she supposed. He grunted and did this tired bison close-his-eyes-and-shake-his-head move, like he could just wish that information away by concentrating real hard.

She had this thought that she could reach out to Ryan, get them together. How long can two people stay mad at each other? She had never been able to tell whether their vibe was dad and son, or like big brother and little brother, just friends, or what. Maybe the closer a relationship gets to feeling like family, the harder it is. Maybe she could get in touch, though, like through a manager or something. Broker a summit.

But then, when headlines about Ryan began to infect her news feeds—*Orland Accused of Drugging, Sexually Assaulting Fan*— she didn't know whether Rudy would want to know: whether he thought Ryan was an asshole and would want to see it confirmed, or still thought he was an OK guy and would want to know he wasn't, or still thought he's an OK guy and would feel bad for him.

She didn't know which she'd prefer. Rudy was a smart guy, but he was stubborn enough to ignore things he could see.

Anyway, Ryan's shows in Atlanta were cancelled, which was good for them, crowd-wise? She knew that was kind of a gross way to think about it. But it was kind of a gross situation.

THEY STOPPED IN Austin at the Barton Springs pool. Lily handed Rudy her phone. The first thing he noticed was how exhausted Ryan looked in the pictures accompanying the headlines: eyes baggy, a few streaks of silver in his hair. Lily dove into the clear water while Rudy read.

The story had originated on, of all places, a Mormon forum, where a topical furor over what a church elder had called "nonconsensual immorality" had spilled over into a long and contentious thread on what worldly music was appropriate for Laurels. *I was on mission,* wrote username Abish, *with a woman who had her virtue besmirched by a "rock star."*

> She had stopped following the Word of Wisdom, and she made some friends who found it funny to tempt her into sin. They took her to a Ryan Orland show in St. Louis, where she and her friend were drugged and brought to his hotel room, and he defiled them.
>
> The shame of her participation in this fornication brought her back to the church. This was fifteen years ago, and she finally found the strength to bear her testimony.
>
> I share this to expose the deception of the idolatry brought to bear on this man who soweth to his flesh; the immorality and hypocrisy of a man whose fame and public image is premised on his sensitivity and his vulnerability, which he obviously deploys as a lure to the unsuspecting Young Women.
>
> I believe the sister.

A *HAYSTACK* NEWS editor with a vigilant search alert wrote up the accusation. The orthodox response—*believe women*—was complicated by suspicion of the appropriation of the movement to the service of a narrative of the immorality of pop music, not to mention a reflexive distrust of a community run by literal patriarchs.

The controversy over the source of the story only fueled its spread. Ryan's name stayed in the headlines of op-eds, contrarian defenses, and meta takes. Phone videos of people taking a seam ripper to their Ryan Orland patches or effacing their lyric tattoos chattered across the commons. Ryan's new record, *At The Pass*, was put on hold; the single, "Let X=X and Solve for Why," pulled from distribution. (Ryan would never grow out of these puns, Rudy thought; then, I guess the song about me wasn't the single after all.) In his brief statement—he didn't know either of these women, this kind of thing was utterly against his principles and his convictions—Ryan sounded not just defensive, but betrayed. He had filled his emotional world with his fans (friends, he probably would have called them, at least at first), his network of virtual or imagined or projected confidants. But the pack had turned, and was now in full cry.

Rudy felt—what did he feel? A bland, headshaking disapproval, though not quite disappointment or disgust. A bleak satisfaction at the defeat of a friend's stubborn optimism: welcome to the lethargy of the soul, the moral torpor. A dissociated gloating: now you're the asshole. Welcome to the abject sublime.

He'd left his sunglasses in the van, and his brow was sore with squinting. He put Lily's phone down on the moist concrete. He hadn't wanted to strip and swim, but he opened two buttons on his shirt in a small concession to blossoming sweat.

Lily bloomed up out of the water and mopped open her hair.

"I feel like I just washed my soul," she said, wrapping herself in a towel. "You gotta go in. Do you good."

Rudy shook his head. "I don't like how it feels, putting on socks after I go swimming. Squinching them over wet feet, bits of dirt and mud. Feel it the rest of the day."

"That's a really stupid reason not to go swimming."

Rudy didn't dispute that: "Easier to just indulge my own idiocies." He looked up at her, and quickly away—the sun's corona burned around her dark face.

"So, how about your asshole buddy?" she asked.

"Hmm," said Rudy.

"You knew the guy. Did you know he was like this?"

"Like what?"

"A scumbag with women."

Rudy rebuttoned his shirt. "Is that what he is?"

"You read what they're saying." Lily pulled her jeans up over her still-wet bathing suit bottom. "Shit—is that why you guys don't talk any more?" She looked at him with something like admiration.

"Not—" Rudy said, and stopped. "No. Something like that."

"Well, good on you," she said. "Cut those people out like a cancer."

"It's not that simple."

"It's not?"

He got up. "I think I'm gonna write him."

She looked at him, hand on her zipper. "Are you fucking kidding me? Now?

"He's my friend."

"He's not your friend."

"He's something."

RUDY PICKED UP a brass music box from the cluttered junk-shop shelf. Ryan had responded almost immediately to his email—curt, but not rude. He was holed up in a hotel nearby; he'd meet Rudy at the front bar of the venue after Rudy's sound check. Fiveish. Rudy could picture him: curtains drawn, searching his own name in a spasm of masochism, refreshing comments, swallowing denunciations, composing and not posting justifications, chipping away at the conviction of his irresistibility. People who love you for the things you make, their love is conditional. You have to win it over and over again, without end, refresh it, plead for it. Not like family, who you have to work to drive away.

Whatever decorative shell had once concealed the mechanism of the music box had been stripped away. The pock-marked cylinder lay on its side, sidled up against the caressing tines of the comb. Two shiny screws looked up inquisitively. Rudy spun the arm, and a short, twinkling melody played, then repeated. A simple machine. The perfect performer.

Would it be arrogant of him to claim some portion of Ryan's success, and the people to whom Ryan's music meant so much, for himself, as part of his own work? Not that he meant to appropriate Ryan's songs, or his person; but he had it in him to relish Ryan's success and not to envy it, to see himself clear, as one who handed a rock and laid a little mortar, to accept his place as he was ranked by the world. As a performer, Ryan had been his better. Lauren, Cass, innumerable strangers could clearly see that, and had been telling him for years. Everyone's blind spot is themselves.

Parents and children can come into conflict and competition, but one, eventually, must yield and take pride in the other's achievements. He had wallowed in the luxury of envy—*he who has no house can rail against great buildings*—but Ryan's humbling had unexpectedly awakened in him a fierce vigilance on Ryan's behalf that was not entirely unselfish. Was the instinct of a parent to defend their child solely on the child's behalf, or, just a little, a defense of the part of them that lives in the child? Was that dishonorable?

Rudy had to laugh at himself—he was letting the prose of his thoughts off the leash, sailing past purple in search of a majestic ultraviolet. As if he wasn't just another person who had discovered himself to be simply a minor artist. *They talk about the sorrows of great artists, the tragic unhappiness of great artists*—a line he had read and remembered—*but after all they are great artists. A little artist has all the tragic unhappiness and the sorrows of a great artist and he is not a great artist.* At least failure couldn't be commodified. Failure, the last refuge.

But—a reduced Ryan was a Ryan to whom he had something to offer. Who needed him, again. An old friend, returning when everyone else shunned him, offering not absolution, just compassion and sorrowful judgment. That was an image Rudy liked.

"FUCKING BARBARIANS," said Ryan, keeping his eyes on the TV mounted over the end of the bar. "You lose a kid in a war, they give you a fucking gold star, like you did a great job copying the alphabet off the blackboard. Fucking condescending."

It was already darkening on the front patio. A couple of men were sitting at tables by themselves, waiting for the kitchen to open. A slice of Hammond cheese burbled from the radio. The remaining sun shone between crossed beams from a single skylight. A shelf high on the wall displayed old tin serving trays with bright bold beer logos.

Ryan was bent-shouldered over a stool, a gray hood pulled over his forehead as far as it would go. The ingratiating whippet diplomat had gone sallow. He held a pint of seltzer, with a cloudy burst of bitters, with both hands, fingers interlocked. Rudy pulled out the stool next to him, the screech briefly shocking in the quiet room.

Mostly what he felt was pity, and a protectiveness: resentment was his weight to carry, so that Ryan could remain the immaculate idealist. To hear even a hint of his own bitterness in Ryan seemed to him a tragedy.

"One summer in college," Rudy said, "I got a job at a resort in the Catskills, one of those lefty folk-song camps. Like a Fresh Air Fund for old Jews out of the Soviet Union. There were two groups of them, though: the ones who left after Trotsky and were still loyal to their idea of what the Soviet Union could have been, and the ones Brezhnev let out, who hated Communism. Every night we had to run this activity, a structured discussion about current events. And every night, we'd have fifty old people in chairs in a circle raising their hands and yelling at each other about things that happened seventy years before."

"Are you trying to open with a parable about holding grudges?" Ryan turned and looked at him for the first time.

"I'm trying to say I'm sorry. I don't want to keep marinating in the past."

"Nice that you can exonerate yourself," Ryan said. "The world thinks I'm a moral monster, and you want to make sure to let me know in person that you're not mad at me anymore? Say something to them."

"Me? To whom?"

"Anyone. The press. A statement."

"A statement?"

"You're a coward. You don't want your name anywhere near this."

"No, it's just—who would care what I say, like if I vouched for you? Who the hell am I?"

"You're the one who was there."

Rudy flushed in a wave. "The fuck are you talking about. You know, my niece is furious that I'm even talking to you."

"Your niece?" Ryan loosened the strings from around his throat and pulled back his hood. "Fuck, never mind. And you're squeaky clean, huh? You let her think that."

"Whatever you did with that girl, that's on you."

"That girl?" Ryan said. "Did you even read what she wrote?"

"I read an article. Those stories, they're vague, they could mean all kinds of things, Ryan, but none of them praiseworthy. I don't want to know that shit about you."

"I suppose nothing about a Mormon girl in St. Louis sounds like anyone you know." A bartender came to offer Rudy a drink. He opened his mouth to order a beer, but Ryan brusquely waved her away. "You know whose story that is? That's you and me, that night. You remember. That's someone who heard that girl, what's-her-name, Selima's friend, talking about her weird wild night with big rock star Ryan Orland and doesn't know who the fuck you are and left you out of the story." He spit on the floor. "So you can take all those times you got mad for being confused with me or like folded up into me and throw them in the fucking trash, 'cause we are even for-fucking-ever."

A sick ember stoked and glowed in Rudy's gut. "That's not what happened."

"Isn't it?" asked Ryan. "How isn't that what happened?"

"She didn't—"

"You know what's funny?" said Ryan. "I don't even know what happened in that room after I left. Sounds like *you* did something you shouldn't have done. What did you do, Rudy?"

"Nothing, I—"

"Stop. It's my turn to be the one who doesn't want to know. It doesn't even matter. Whatever you did, one of those girls felt like you shouldn't have."

Rudy didn't say anything.

"I never used to do any of that rock star bullshit," said Ryan. "All that spoils-of-war dick swinging, I thought it was stupid. Old-fashioned. Fuck that. I never thought I was better or bigger than anyone who came to see me. And people talk, now; it's not like anything stays behind closed doors. When people are like, how come there's no more *real rock stars* anymore, it's like, well, there's not enough money and there's a hell of a lot more decency. But when I saw how Jules was with girls, and then you—I don't know, you weren't like some guitar god from the mythic past, you were just a guy I knew, a guy I respected. I was still looking to you for direction. I left that room, but I wasn't sure—I felt like maybe I was missing out on something, or I wasn't doing rock-star right, or like you were signing off on it. So next time I came through town, I did call Selima, and then some others after that, and it was easier every time. And then I'm in peoples', like, stories 'cause I'm famous or whatever, and you know what happens to stories, and fucking—here we are. I'm not trying to let myself off the hook. I've done stuff I'm not proud of. But that was a door you opened for me. Sure, I learned some things about playing and singing and writing from you. But I also learned how to act." He pulled his hood back up. "So many rules you have to learn, coming up—wear this, don't say that; but also, we make our own rules, the straight world's rules don't apply here in our little freedom fantasy. A world of ethics but no morals. Eighteen-year-olds telling the four-teens how to live, twenty-threes giving advice to the seventeens, thirty-threes talking down to the twenty-fives. Pass it on. Around and around. Just a circle of jerks."

Rudy turned away first. Stared at the dusty spire of Galliano, just to have somewhere else to look, but Ryan's sunken eyes were waiting for him in the mirror.

"You don't know it was that night," he murmured.

"But I can tell," Ryan said, "that you think it was."

"I can't help you."

"You could."

"How would that look? A nobody pops up to take the fall for the rock star, the guy he depends on for his career, the guy most people credit for his very existence? I'll look like your paid-off patsy. Nobody will buy that."

"I'll ask you again. Help me."

"Lily. My niece. She respects me. She's the only one—now—who does."

"So, you won't."

"What else do I have, after twenty-five years of this, but what she thinks of me?"

Ryan spread his arms and turned to both sides. "What else do *I* have? You know, I didn't talk to my mother for five years after I left home. She hit me up for money once. Then she passed. The one time I reached out to my dad, he called me a pussy. This is all I have, too."

"You've got three houses," said Rudy. "That I know of. I live in my car half the year."

"That's—honestly—not why I've ever done this. I'm thirty-three. It's not enough to live on the rest of my life."

The bartender discreetly placed a pint of water in front of Rudy.

"You're going to leave," said Ryan. "You're just going to let me take it."

The silence ballooned and popped. "Yes."

Ryan pushed a twenty-dollar bill parallel to the glass rail. "Congratulations," he said. "You got what you wanted. How does it feel?"

"This isn't what I wanted," said Rudy.

Ryan looked back at Rudy. "Once, I hoped we'd be on the same team. I found out you don't do teams. I thought you were like a brother. But you're not that, either. Family doesn't do this to each other."

"I have family," said Rudy.

"Nice for you," said Ryan. "Don't worry. I won't blow your cover."

"I'm sorry."

"Are you?" Ryan got up from his stool. "You liked me all right, once. Not enough to care. Remember, in my basement? You said, this stuff is hard." He pulled up his hood. "Writing songs is easy. It's everything else that's hard."

"SO," SAID LILY. She folded a T-shirt into a neat display square, and set it on the folding table. "Were you the priest or the executioner?"

Rudy felt drained and pinned, spread and exposed, a butterfly mounted on cork. Flattened in minutes from magnanimous to supplicant. Habit and instinct told him to mutter an evasion: it was OK, it was weird, let's go get some dinner. Lily, though— she deserved more than a euphemism for a lie. And she'd know anyway, and judge him for it, even if she didn't call him on it; this tough, sharp young woman, this child who—come to think of it— wouldn't exist if not for him. He'd failed Ryan. He owed her more.

And he owed penance—whether to Ryan, or to himself, or to— something, wasn't yet clear.

"I had never considered," he said, "the idea of a black mark on one's soul, as anything other than a cliché. But it's horrifying. If you start as a clean slate, I mean, then what are those black marks, but the writing that describes your character. What if a person is entirely made of those black marks. The book of your soul."

"You getting religious on me?" she said.

Rudy looked away. "Call it what you want. Augustine spent a year sleeping around and the rest of his life feeling bad about it, and half the world followed his lead for the next fifteen hundred years." The secular age, he said, we still haven't found a way to accommodate the persistence of transgression in the human animal. What are our institutions of expiation? Rituals of repentance; contrition, confession, penance—but where now was the priest who could give absolution?

Lily re-capped a marker and stuck it in the fanny pack that doubled as cashbox, zipped the pocket closed. "Well, I haven't heard him try to defend himself. Maybe he's got some things he feels like he needs to atone for." Ryan, she said, seems like the kind of guy who will get through this. He'll sense the right amount of time to keep his head down, the right tone to strike when he comes back, and then he'll have this extra layer of depth because he'll feel like a guy who's been through some shit. Finally shed that spiritual baby fat. What people love even more than turning on someone is taking them back. "There's your religious angle," she said. "You, focus on tonight, and tomorrow, and next week." She pushed a cardboard box under the table. "And Mom wants you to call her about Grandpa."

"I used to have a line, when I was twenty, twenty-one, that all I had were regrets of inaction. Like, my life isn't interesting enough, I wish I had—just do this thing, or the other, what's the worst that could happen, get a good story out of it. I said—in total sincerity—that from now on, I wanted all my regrets to be regrets of action, not inaction. People—Ryan—would nod, like, oh, yeah, totally, badass. Now it seems like the worst advice imaginable."

Lily looked at him carefully, as if at a child crying because they'd knocked their smaller sibling off a couch, who needed to be both chastised and comforted. "I guess you're not talking about Ryan," she said.

SO RUDY TOLD her the whole story, and she listened, and left, after a while, for a while.

He had to get used to being stuck with himself again, with the chafe of conscience where once lay the comforting wool-blanket prickle of resentment. But without the spur of confidence, or truculence, or presumption, or pique, he could no longer locate a justification to step on stage. *Cherish your grudges*, Seb had said: *if you lose everything else, they'll give you a reason to get out of bed.* The shows felt—pointless. What was he trying to prove, now? All the shards of pain and promise that had prodded him on had melted away before he'd been able to mend them, mold them into something.

He turned on the radio: a politician's just-so fable; a cretin defrocked. Ethical degenerates peddling psychic decay in the offices of power and the paper megaphones of personal media. Morally disabled men to emulate. Lily was right: it was a kind of triumph just to live.

He tried to repair the situation from a distance, though not very hard. He roused to contact Selima, but her phone number was now in the hands of someone speaking what might have been Mandarin. Elin—he didn't even know her last name. Besides, he couldn't fix this from backstage. He'd been too craven to expose himself when he'd had his chance to help Ryan, and the chance wouldn't come again. Anything else was mopping up the water without turning off the hose.

He turned to his remaining reliable comfort—aimless driving, as if he could outpace or elude the telling of his own story. Up: hills broken and upended, their striations pointing skyward; a lumpy, frosted popover mountain. Down: fog insulated the valley. A moldy, avocado-colored canal moving imperceptibly if at all. Old men fishing. A lethargic cluster of boarded-up villas, rotting plaster walls, tan and tile, palm and cypress. He stopped to eat lunch by a map-promised brook, but the hurricane-lashed river had not just jumped its banks, but rewritten them. The riverbend now shrank to the far end of a floodplain as if recoiling from his presence, as if he'd parched and seared the bed, exposed the skeletal stumps, the flapping choking fish.

He removed the folder of Lily's letters from his guitar case, as if they were beloved relics that, too, could be poisoned by his proximity. He sat on the bank, folded them into hatlike boats, and launched them one by one, sacrificial offerings with a retinue of polliwogs. Some toppled and sank; most managed to skirt the snag, ripple sideways, swirl over a patch of whitewater and escape rushing downriver; one was trapped circling in a miniature whirlpool for a while before it saturated and drowned.

25

THIS TIME, Rudy told Lauren, it made sense that he be the one to go look after their father.

Lauren was prepping for her semester and Lily was about to start school. Olivia and Charles had been forced to sell the Madison house. A former student of Charles's had offered them the vacation use of a cabin she had inherited, north of Toronto, off Lake Huron. It had been built as a summer camping lodge, but they'd weatherized it—to a point—and now, her charity extended, they moved there, it seemed, permanently. Olivia was exhausted by years of caring for her deteriorating husband. Her widowed sister in California had invited her to come visit, indefinitely—"until she felt better"—and Olivia wanted to accept. "It's something," Rudy said, "that I can do for the family. What do I have planned that's so important?"

You only get a few people in life, he said, who care about you despite yourself—despite everything you've done to make them not care. Cass couldn't care anymore. Ryan doesn't care anymore. You do, somehow. Mom and Dad still care. See if I can't prove them, finally, right.

"Well, I'm glad to hear this from you," said Lauren. "Somehow I recognize the argument. Could have come earlier."

Rudy wanted to apologize, but couldn't quite figure out how. "I'm sorry," he said.

"Lily cares, too. You took care of her. I'm grateful to you for that."

"Yes," said Rudy. "I did. But I suppose it's not something you have to do just once."

Imagine there's a straight line, he said, that represents how you ought to be in the world, a median standard of behavior. And then imagine another line—not a line, an embodied motion, approaching and fleeing your ideal like a flock of starlings around a telephone pole, a murmuration of the soul into—for lack of a better word—sin, then back into goodness, folding and layering. They never land, the two never reconcile; and the past is always pulling away, not with force, but with assiduity. The best you can do is try to average out to decency. Or to grab onto that pole as you fly by, and wrap yourself around it.

RUDY HADN'T REPLACED his temporary passport. He went to the post office and filled out an application.

"Have you had a passport before?" asked the clerk.

"Yeah," said Rudy. "Got ripped off." He handed over the sweat-blistered replacement, and the clerk paper clipped it to the sheaf of papers and dropped the package in a manila envelope.

"Have you had your identity stolen?"

"Thought I had, but it was a false alarm."

HE DROVE LILY to school like closing a circle. Back in the South, where he'd lived with Cass, where Lily's parents had met, where— he guessed—Seb still prowled. Where his life had, apparently, really begun; where the forces, anyway, that nudged or propelled him had originated; the way a star was born, coalesced impercep-tibly from inchoate chaos, as particles—each with their own direc-tion, charge, properties, attractions, repulsions—collided. Forces morally neutral in themselves. Only what passed through a human could become good or bad.

A star! That was a good one.

"Drop me off on the plaza," she said, and he pulled up by the benches.

The column had been removed and updated. In its place was a two-sided digital billboard rotating exhibitions, concerts, propa-ganda, public notices; blaring green, red, white, green again. Faces sprang into life, even into motion, then blinked out of existence. Someone had taped a paper flyer onto the chrome edge; it had almost finished curling off. A pigeon hop-fluttered to a perch on its top edge and pecked at a dry seed. The clock on a small inset screen flashed 12:00, 12:00, 12:00. Rudy felt like it was costing him his last reserves of energy to leave Lily there. He squeezed her forearm and withdrew his hand through the driver's-side window.

"Mister sentimental," she said.

"I'd say don't fuck it up," said Rudy, "but—"

"I'll try not to do anything irreversible."

"Best you can hope." He started the car.

"If you find anything cool at Grandpa's, send it to me."

"C'mon. Don't be a ghoul."

Lily laughed. "OK, fine. I don't want any of his junk anyway."

"Do you want—" He hesitated, then pointed a thumb at his guitar case in the back seat. "Would you have any use for that?"

She started to smile; it passed through a smirk before she suppressed it with a twitch. "No," she said. "I don't." She picked up her backpack and the handle of her suitcase. "What do you think you'll do, while you're up there?"

236 · someone should pay for your pain

"For now," said Rudy, "nothing. Probably just stay there a while. See if I can stand my own company. Talk to Dad when he's awake. Live quietly, and try not to be called anything worse than my name."

acknowledgments

This book would not have been possible without residencies at the Ucross Foundation and the Holy Cross Monastery.

No working parent would ever complete anything without assistance, and I want to acknowledge the affectionate care of Sara Foglia, Anne-Mieke de Wild, Eleanor Robb, Maddie Hopfield, Izzy Spain, Sienna Thompson, David Romtvedt & Margo Belem, and the wonderful teachers at the Bard Nursery School, each of whom helped raise my children while I wrote this book.

Thanks to Jay Stringer for inviting me to write the story that became the genesis of the book; and to readers who provided incisive and invaluable feedback, especially (though not exclusively) Philip Anderson, Daphne Palasi Andreades, Patti Yumi Cottrell, Jean Kyoung Frazier, Erroll McDonald, Paul La Farge, Rivka Galchen, Eli Gottlieb, Sam Lipsyte, Ben Metcalf, Peter Michalik, Lee Siegel, Darcey Steinke, Lara Vapnyar, and Emily Meg Weinstein.

Matt Walker's *Gainesville Punk* was a useful source for imagining the Expats' milieu, though of course their town overlaps only in a general sense with the actual place, and is mostly fantastical in its specifics.

Much gratitude to John Silbersack, Sarah Fan, and Deborah Robertson for taking chances on my writing.

The love and support of Franz C. Nicolay, Susan Lirakis, Megan Nicolay, Sophie Nicolay, Ariana Nicolay, Chrystia Sonevytsky, Marko & Allie Sonevytsky, and the rest of my extended family have been a reliable and treasured foundation.

And, of course, everything is for Maria, Lesia, and Artem.